Wicked Distractions

WICKED TROUBLE

ANGELA ADDAMS

Wicked Trouble
ISBN # 978-1-83943-778-6
©Copyright Angela Addams 2022
Cover Art by Fiona Jayde ©Copyright March 2022
Interior text design by Claire Siemaszkiewicz
Totally Bound Publishing

Totally Bound Publishing books by Angela Addams

Single Books
Forever My Cowboy
Must Love Cats

Wicked Distractions
Wicked Disclosure
Wicked Ways
Wicked Secrets
Wicked Trouble

Collections
Naughty or Nice?: Wicked Christmas

WICKED TROUBLE

Dedication

I'm dedicating this book to Jamie Rose, editor extraordinaire and the reason this story exists.

Chapter One

Cammie didn't do vacations very well, mostly because she loathed stepping away from the love of her life…work. But when the uber-powerful Sabine Cowan insisted on an all-expenses paid kink cruise, what she called *"mandatory R and R"*, what was a girl supposed to do?

A hardcore type-A like Cammie played to her strengths, so that's what she did. She packed her bags and made a cruise 'to-do' list. One, schmooze and network more Kitty Cat connections—Gentlemen's Club candidates, Kitty Cat hopefuls and new clients. Two, product test, because, come on…a kink cruise? *A girl's gotta have a little fun at work.* Three, get laid…repeatedly. *It is a vacation after all…even if it's forced.* It'd been a looong time since she'd found a man to crank her little kink-loving heart.

"This will be your cabin, Miss Sheppard. Your boss really loves you." Ben, her steward, winked like they were already best friends. He'd been effervescent the entire way to her stateroom, bubbling with energy and peppering her with questions about where she'd traveled from and what she hoped to do on the five-day cruise. It had been impossible not to get caught up in his enthusiasm as he pumped up the various events that had been planned. "Shall I put your bags in the closet?"

A walk-in closet? In a stateroom? "Yes, please. Thank you, Ben."

Of course, Sabine had spared no expense, so Cammie's cabin was beyond luxurious. It was larger than her own bedroom at home in New York and big enough for a king-size bed, a lounge-dining area and a restroom that included an actual whirlpool tub. The view was spectacular as well. With floor-to-ceiling windows along one wall, Cammie would be able to see miles of ocean with no obstructed views. She also had a balcony and pictured herself having her morning coffee there while she checked email and knocked a few things off her 'non-cruise to-do list', of course.

"Is there anything else I can do for you, Miss Sheppard?" Ben stood at the door, his hands folded in front of him and his face clearly eager to please. His blond hair flopped over one eye, giving him an adorably disheveled look.

"Oh gosh, no. I'm fine." She dug out some money from her purse then handed it to him. "Thanks for getting me here safe and sound. This ship is so huge. I think it'll take me five days just to get the hang of where everything is." Which was a total lie… Cammie had gotten the entire ship mapped out from bow to stern and everything in between before she'd stepped foot on board.

"I'm here if you need me. Just pick up the phone and I'll answer." Ben slipped the cash into his pocket with a nod and a grin. "Don't forget about the sunset mixer on the Sky Deck."

Cammie rubbed her hands together. "I'll be there!" A sunset mixer sounded like exactly the type of place she'd find people to network with.

She had an hour to get ready, so she pulled out her sun-and-fun mixer dress—an orange, yellow and pink strapless that hugged her curves just right—then headed into the massive restroom for a dip in the tub. If Sabine wanted her to relax, she could at least make an effort.

It turned out that networking was easier than finding a nonalcoholic cocktail on the Sky Deck. Cammie had been offered no less than four umbrella-adorned drinks by four different scantily clad servers, and each time she'd asked if it was possible to get a soda or even water, she'd only been met with looks of confusion before a mumbled, "Of course! Let me get that for you." She'd yet to find a cold drink in her hand, but she had met three very eligible men, who had been eagerly listening to what she had to say about the Kitty Cat Gentlemen's Club. They hadn't even balked at the fee range she'd hinted at.

"You can sign me up, little lady." Mr. William Haversmith wore a huge tan cowboy hat on his big head. Everything about the man was larger than life, from his booming laugh and his ridiculously large cowboy boots to his long, curled mustache. "In fact, a pretty little thing like you can do whatever she wants with my assets." He winked.

"Bill, don't you know women don't like to be spoken to like that?" Elm Stone also wore a cowboy hat and towered over Cammie in the same way his friend did, which wasn't hard, considering Cammie was a whopping five foot three inches. He tried to come off as more gentlemanly, even though Cammie had witnessed him slip his hands over several of the servers' asses as they passed by.

"I'm sorry. Can't help myself. You're a tiny, sexy thing, though. And on a naughty cruise like this to boot! You're a firecracker, aren't you? I can see it in your eyes." He winked again, and Cammie had to wonder if he had a tic or if he really did think she — or any woman, really — was in to his kind of flirting. "And those dimples! So cute! I could just eat you up." He leaned closer. "You don't mind if I call you 'little lady', do you, sweetheart?"

Did she mind? *Hell yes!* But she'd never say that out loud. Working in an industry that catered to men, she'd become used to the ways that men behaved and the condescending things they often said. "Of course not, Mr. Haversmith." She grinned, making sure her dimples popped for him. "I'm just going to charge you more for your membership."

The men all laughed in their hearty way, not believing for one second that she would, in fact, give them the elevated price she reserved for special men like him. She laughed too, but hers — if a person listened closely — was edged with a 'fuck you'.

"Well, you've got my contact information. Be sure to put it to good use, honey." He didn't wink again, *thank goodness*, but he did waggle his eyebrows like he was sending some kind of secret message.

Cammie laughed again then waved him off. "If you'll excuse me, gentlemen, I'm going to search out a drink. I'm absolutely parched!" She didn't stick around for another suggestive comment, but the men's laughter and what could only be described as catcalls did follow her as she moved through the crowd.

Ugh.

"Oh, there you are!" A tall redhead wearing a super-flattering, black skin-hugging leather dress rushed to her on four-inch stilettos with a frosty glass in hand. "Soda water for you. I added a lime just in case you wanted a bit of flavor."

"Thank you!" The timing couldn't have been more perfect. Cammie really was dying of thirst.

"Soda water, huh?"

She turned toward the gravelly voice like a puppet on a string. "Yeah, I'm not in to alcohol."

"Smart. Don't want to get too drunk then end up tied down and at some Dom's mercy." The guy standing next to her checked all Cammie's eye-candy boxes. He was tall and wide, barrel-chested, thick-armed and, like her, appeared to enjoy food. "That's why I'm only sipping my beer."

"Bound and at the mercy of a Dom is exactly how I want to end up." A bold statement, sure, but Cammie had a to-do list, and this guy might be her way to check off one of those bullet points.

"Zane," he said, one eyebrow raised.

Amused or intrigued? It was hard to tell. He tilted his pint glass toward hers.

"Cammie." She turned herself toward him so she could take in his full size then clinked her glass with his. She liked men with meat on them. They complemented her curves and were usually hefty enough to hoist her into the positions she loved. "You here alone?"

His eyes crinkled and a grin tugged his lips. "Are you hitting on me?"

"Not yet." Cammie grinned back.

"Oh...dimples, how very —"

"If you say cute, I'm leaving." Cammie took a sip from her glass, watching him over the jutting lime. Her body heat had to be wafting off her with the way her pussy quivered and wept. Zane was exactly the kind of guy she could have some fun with.

Get laid – check!

"Enticing." He gave her a spicy once-over, trailing a hot-as-hell gaze down, lingering over her double Ds to the curve of her extra-wide hips, then back up again. "Yes, I'm here alone."

"I'm not looking for love." Cammie would never be accused of beating around the bush, especially not when it came to sex.

"Neither am I."

* * * *

Smack!

Cammie's ass burned like a thousand suns, and she was sure that Zane's handprint would be seared into her flesh before he was done with her. He had taken her over his knee, and, as she'd correctly guessed, he was hefty enough to lift, then hold her there while he squeezed her dangling tits and walloped her cheeks with his open palm. Neither of them had wasted time stripping, and his hearty cock was digging into her stomach, nudging her every time Zane reeled back for another hit. She would have liked to rub his shaft, but he'd expertly tied her hands behind her back using her bra, and she wasn't in a position to maneuver his cock into her mouth. She was at this bear's mercy, just as she liked it.

Not for the first time, Zane seemed to read her mind. He heaved her off his lap then positioned her on her knees. He spread his legs, his cock jutting massively at mouth level. "Let me see those dimples pop, dirty girl."

She grinned as she opened her mouth then gulped down his dick, pressing her tongue firmly to his shaft as he eased his way in. She gagged and he pulled back, but she shook her head, opened her mouth wider, shifted forward, then took him all the way into her throat.

He growled like a predator that was hungry for more. She sucked him as she moved all the way back to his tip, her lips pressed around his head, flicking her tongue along the ridge of his crown. He reached down to fondle her breasts, pulling a yelp out of her as he pinched and pulled her nipples until her eyes watered.

She swallowed his cock, taking him to the hilt, then slowly backing off again. He smacked her tits with a sharp slap, angling to hit the sides so that they slammed together. He'd squeeze them, gripped hard before moving back to her nipples, tweaking and taunting them all over again.

He spurted a drop of cum, like a preshow to the big explosion, and Cammie swallowed it greedily. She wanted more but he pushed her back so forcefully that she landed on her sore ass with a thump and moaned through the smarting pain.

"We're coming together." He lifted her by the underarms, then flipped her over, shoving her face-down into the mattress.

She heard more than saw him rip open a condom package and her core coiled. She lifted her ass and buried her face into the comforter.

Smack!

Her ass burned all over again. She gulped down a scream.

Smack!

She rocked forward on a groan.

He nudged her legs wider, slipped his hand around her waist and hoisted her up and back, before spearing her completely with his giant dick.

She gasped but he gave her no time to adjust. Instead, he swatted her ass again and again, each hit punctuated by a thrust of his rock-hard cock.

He reached around and rubbed her clit, sending explosive sparks through her body. Her toes curled and her pussy spasmed. She dug her shoulder into the bed to keep her face from being smothered and gazed behind to watch this beast of a man ram her. He rocked her with his powerful thrusts, teased her into a frenzy with his fingers circling her clit so roughly and, somehow, continued to tan her ass, alternating between sides until she was sure she'd never be able to sit again.

His dick was a steel rod — hard, slick and punishing as he drilled her relentlessly. Her self-control was no match for his unwavering attention, so when her orgasm crested, holding back was impossible. There'd be no delayed gratification today. Her climax spasmed through her with a full body quiver, then cascaded like a rocket launcher, shooting blast after blast until she was crying out through each shockwave. Zane bellowed through his orgasm, grunting and groaning with each thrust until he collapsed to his knees, sliding his cock out of her pussy before she was completely finished with him. He kissed her sore ass cheeks, and his tenderness made her knees wobble.

She shifted to her side, too scared to put weight on her ass right away, and looked down at him. He brushed his fingers through his hair, pushing it from his face as he puffed out his breaths.

"You done?" she asked with a quirk of her lips. "Or are you hungry for more?"

His eyes narrowed in that sexy hooded way men had. "I'm always hungry for more."

"I think every cabin has suspension gear in the closet." She motioned to his smaller, more cost-efficient space where some of his clothes appeared to be hanging. His cabin was several floors down from hers and was more like a dorm room—tight space and plain decor. "I don't think I'll be able to sit for a while."

"I'm good at tying knots." Zane pulled the condom from his cock before standing. "And there are hooks all over this room." Which made the tight space all-the-more appealing. He could literally suspend her over the bed if he wanted—and she definitely wanted.

"Then I think we're in for a really fun night."

* * * *

Somehow, in the haze of her post-climax buzz, Cammie found her way through the maze of decks to her cabin. It was too early for anyone to be out and about. Even the crew was virtually non-existent at three a.m. Cammie was very much looking forward to pouring herself into bed and sleeping the rest of the morning away. *Breakfast be damned.* Her appetite had been satiated already—repeatedly, in fact.

She slipped her key card into the reader, thankful when it beeped without a fuss, then slipped quietly into her room. The view of the ocean and how it kissed the star-infused night sky was breathtaking. Cammie didn't bother turning on the lights. She could see the bed and that was the only destination she had in mind.

She took a few steps then stumbled, her foot catching on something solid next to the bed. Luckily, she braced herself on the night table so she didn't hit the floor.

"What the…?" She flicked on the light and shifted an annoyed look to whatever had tripped her.

Then she choked on a scream.

Lying next to her bed, on the floor, was a man. He was on his back, his face slack, his mouth gaping and his eyes wide and vacant.

He was clearly, very definitely dead.

Chapter Two

Of all the cases Zane had worked in the last year since becoming a private investigator, this one, by far, was the best—not only because he was on a cruise ship with an all-you-can-eat buffet that was a mile long or because a fetish cruise was right up his dark pleasure alley. No, those things were definitely perks, but working this case meant that he'd be able to indulge in the vivacious, sexy and totally delicious Cammie Sheppard. He counted himself extremely lucky to have met her right out of the gate, considering that they'd clicked instantly—explosive chemistry right from hello.

Cammie had only left an hour before, but her ginger-mandarin scent lingered to a distracting degree. Zane wanted to give her a call in her cabin and tell her how much he'd enjoyed their time together, but he didn't want to come off as clingy or desperate. Besides, breakfast was only a few hours away, another all-you-can-eat bonanza, and he had plans to meet up with her there.

Okay...he hadn't actually made plans *with* her to meet her there, but the idea had just occurred to him, so he figured he could swoop by her stateroom and rouse her out of bed so they could go together.

He logged into the cruise's crew database and scrolled through the pictures. His job was to sniff out a thief—or a ring of thieves more likely—since there was over a million dollars missing, taken in small increments spanning at least six trips through the Bahamas. His job wasn't to confront or to accuse, only to investigate, hopefully find evidence, then turn it all over to Dark Matter's CEO, Cal Underwood. Everyone was a suspect, so Zane had to play the part of a fetish lover and blend in with the crowd.

So far so good in that regard.

Cammie not only helped his cover, but she was hella good at getting him off—and those dimples, whew! Drop-dead heartstopper.

She'd told him right off the bat that she wasn't looking for a commitment or anything serious, so their fling suited him just fine. Although, he wouldn't lie. If their fun kept up for the whole five days of the cruise, he was going to be sad to part ways.

What a hard life.

Zane refocused on the task at hand. He had to create a list based on employees who worked in the various areas where money had been siphoned, who'd also been present on all six trips to the Bahamas over the last six months, and he was technically already behind in his plans.

If he worked his ass off for the next three hours, he'd have just enough time to hop in the shower then get up to Cammie's swanky deck before—

Knock, knock, knock!

"Mr. Roberts, can you please open your door?"

18

Zane frowned. It was four in the morning. *What in the hell is someone doing bugging me now?*

"Sir, it's an emergency. If you would please—"

Zane opened his door to find his steward, Remi, ready to knock again. "What's the emergency?" Unless the ship was sinking, he wasn't in the mood for this kind of drama.

"I-I-I'm sorry if I woke you, M-M-Mr. Roberts," Remi stammered as he took in Zane's lack of shirt and low-slung joggers. "But Captain Evans has requested your immediate presence in his office."

Fuck! Zane blinked back his surprise and tried to play it cool. "Is there a problem?"

"I'm afraid there is, sir, but I'm not at liberty to say. If you could please come with me...er...after you get dressed, of course." Remi gave him a quick once-over, clearly appalled by the informal attire.

Zane was half tempted to insist they go without a change of clothes, but he figured if he was busted, he better at least look like the professional PI that he was trying to be. "Give me a minute."

Remi seemed like he was ready to argue as Zane started to close the door but one arched eyebrow and steely look had the younger man nodding and backing away. "Of course, of course. I'll wait right here for you. But please, Mr. Roberts, hurry."

Shortest investigation ever. Zane wasn't sure how he'd tipped off the captain to his real purpose for being on the ship, but it couldn't have been something he'd said or done. Maybe there was a snitch on board, someone who worked with head office who somehow had discovered Zane's presence on the cruise? Although Cal Underwood had assured him that only the most trusted employees at the head office would know Zane was there and that Cal himself would be the only one who would know exactly why.

He quickly washed his face, slapped on some fresh deodorant then put his kakis on with a button-up that said business casual. He stuffed his feet back into his loafers then joined Remi, who was paler than he had been a few minutes before, in the hallway.

"Lead the way," Zane said with as much of a nonchalant wave of his hand as he could muster. Inside he was reeling, his brain working at hyper-speed to figure out if there was a way to get himself out of this mess and preserve the investigation. Denial would only go so far. If the captain had evidence of some sort… Well, Zane would have to think on his feet, which, luckily, he was relatively good at.

Remi used the most direct route to the captain's office, but it was still ten minutes before Zane found himself standing with sweaty palms and a racing heart on the other side of the door, waiting for Remi to get the go-ahead to enter.

When that actually happened, it was with a stern, "Come in," that sounded more like a command than an invitation and didn't bode well for Zane's future on board the ship.

Do they make people walk the plank these days?

Zane was ready to lead with a deflection strategy in order to buy him some time to figure out what the captain knew about his investigation, but all words dissolved on his tongue the moment he realized that this wasn't a meeting about Zane's work. This was a meeting about Cammie.

She stood on one side of the office, her arms wrapped around herself and her eyes rimmed red. She still wore the clothes she'd had on when she'd left

Zane's cabin an hour before, but now she looked a little more ruffled.

"Mr. Roberts, thank you for coming so quickly," Captain Evans said as he extended his hand. "We've had an incident, and we need to ask you some questions."

Zane shook the man's hand, but his eyes stayed on Cammie. "What kind of incident?" She didn't look hurt, but it was clear she was upset. Her face was pale, the honey hue of her sun-kissed skin completely washed out and her lips quivered just a little, enough to tell him that whatever this incident was, it had affected her more than she was letting on.

"This is my Chief Security Officer, Dilan Ross." Captain Evans motioned to the hulking guy who was standing in the corner. "I'll let him fill you in."

Dilan didn't step forward and only nodded in greeting. He was tall, his back ramrod straight with hands clasped in front of him, definitely military, definitely no nonsense. His head was shaved so close to his scalp that he looked bald, and his eyes were dark and penetrating.

"Miss Sheppard has informed us that she was with you from approximately nine p.m. to approximately three a.m. Is that correct?" Dilan didn't bother to look at Cammie as he spoke about her.

By the way her lips thinned and her eyes narrowed, Zane caught on that her character was in question and that she was pissed.

"Yes, that's correct. We met on the Sky Deck during the sunset mixer then went to my cabin."

"And, to your knowledge, was Miss Sheppard consuming alcohol or drugs during this time? Was she consuming anything that might impact or alter her state of mind?" Dilan said this in a way that suggested he had already formed his conclusions about Cammie's state of mind.

"I've already told you that I don't drink or do drugs," Cammie snipped.

"Miss Sheppard…" Captain Evans winced as he turned his head toward her. "I know this is upsetting for you, but before we can proceed with an investigation—"

"A man is dead—"

"Miss Sheppard, as I've already told you—"

"Whoa! What's going on?" Zane side-stepped Captain Evans and closed the distance between him and Cammie. "What happened?"

"Mr. Roberts—"

Zane held his hand up and gave the Chief of Security a stern look. "If you don't mind, Chief Ross, I'd like to hear what my friend has to say."

The tension Cammie had in her shoulders seemed to ease as he stepped closer to her. "After I left your cabin, I went straight to mine, and when I got inside, there was—" She swallowed a few times, her eyes swimming a little. "There was a man, a dead man, on the floor next to my bed."

"That is what Miss Sheppard has told us," Captain Evans said.

"I'm not following. Are you suggesting that Cammie had something to do with that man's death?" Zane took Cammie's hand and squeezed it before turning to face the captain and his security chief. "Because I can confirm that she was with me and that she didn't, at any point, consume alcohol or drugs, nor did she act in a way that would suggest she had an altered state of mind. When she left my cabin, she was coherent and lucid."

"No, no, Mr. Roberts, we're not suspecting Miss Sheppard of committing murder." Captain Evans gave a dismissive wave. "We're simply trying to establish if it was possible that she maybe could have been hallucinating at the time she returned to her stateroom."

"Hallucinating?" Zane looked from the captain to Cammie then back again.

"When security went to investigate Miss Sheppard's room after she'd notified us of what she'd found, well…" Captain Evans grimaced. "There wasn't a body there at all."

"And no sign of there ever having been a body there," Dilan added.

Zane shook his head. "What? A body doesn't just disappear."

"No, it doesn't, which is why we're simply trying to understand what really happened when Miss Sheppard returned to her room." The captain's attempt at sympathy came across as patronizing. It was clear that he didn't believe her story.

"What really happened was that someone obviously removed the body before you got there." Cammie dropped Zane's hand then moved around him to face off with the captain. "Maybe someone has a reason to hide the body and maybe"—she pointed at Chief Ross—"maybe someone on this ship got rid of it when they were supposed to be confirming what I saw."

"Now, now, Miss Sheppard," Captain Evans said, his hands up as if to calm her. "Let's not make accusations that can't be proven."

"Someone removed the proof from my stateroom!" Cammie yelled.

"I think it might be best if you sleep on it, Miss Sheppard, and we can reconvene in the morning. You're obviously very upset, and I think it's best—"

"Let me get this straight, Captain Evans. You want me to sleep in my room? Where I found a dead man on the floor?" Cammie voice hitched higher with each question. "You want me to sleep it off and hopefully wake up to realize I just imagined tripping over a dead body?"

"Miss Sheppard, please—"

"That's enough." Cammie shook her head as she beelined for the door, sidestepping the captain's attempt to stop her. "I've heard enough." She shot one last glare at the captain then at Dilan before whipping the door open then storming out.

The captain cleared his throat. Dilan arched his eyebrows.

"Did you examine the room thoroughly?" Zane asked.

"There wasn't even a trace of blood or the suggestion of an indent in the carpet," Dilan confirmed. "And there was no body to be seen."

"Mr. Roberts, as the captain of this vessel, I have to assure you that there is nothing on this ship that I don't know about." Captain Evans put his hand on Zane's arm as he guided him toward the door. "Nothing slips past me. So, if a man had died and somehow gotten into Miss Sheppard's room, I'd know about it. Trust me."

Zane always disliked people who demanded trust. In his experience, they always seemed to be the people who were least trustworthy. "Are there security cameras on Miss Sheppard's deck?"

"Yes, yes. Not in the cabin, of course, but Dilan checked the feed and found nothing unusual. No sign of a body being dragged into Miss Sheppard's room — only her steward entering to turn down her sheets."

"And her steward, he's been accounted for?" Zane couldn't make sense of any of this.

"Yes, of course, Ben is fine and didn't see anything untoward happening on Miss Sheppard's deck or the one below that he's in charge of." Captain Evans still held Zane's arm — or tried to anyway — and motioned down the hall. "I wonder if you'd be so kind as to keep an eye on your friend? Make sure she's okay for the remainder of the trip? And, of course, let me know if any new information comes to light?"

Was he being asked to spy on Cammie? He didn't know her well and the evidence didn't add up, but Zane's gut was telling him that something was very off about the captain, *not* Cammie. The man definitely had some secrets of his own...secrets that might be helpful to dig into where Zane's own investigation was concerned.

"I can do that," Zane said.

"Good man!" Captain Evans patted his arm before turning away. "I'll make sure you're comped some extras while you're with us."

And now it felt like a bribe. "That's very thoughtful, thank you."

Captain Evans waved him off. "My gratitude for your empathy. Now, if you don't mind, I have some things to discuss with Dilan. It was a pleasure to meet you, Mr. Roberts."

Zane didn't bother to respond before heading down the hall and away from the captain's office. He needed to get online so he could dig deeper into the crew profiles. There was something very fishy about the captain and his security chief that had Zane's investigative radar pinging — definitely something that might influence his own case.

He didn't get very far before Cammie pounced. She curled her hand under his arm and kept him walking. "We need to talk."

"Hang on." He used his considerably bigger size to halt them both, which forced Cammie to fling back enough to crush against his chest.

"Oof!" She braced herself with both hands on his pecs then looked up like she had no idea why they'd stopped walking.

"Are you okay?" Zane maybe didn't believe one hundred percent that Cammie had seen what she said she had but he did one hundred percent believe that she *believed* she'd seen a dead man on her floor.

Cammie frowned as something that looked a lot like impatience flashed across her face. "Yes. I mean, no. Well, I'm pissed off that no one believes me about what I saw. I'm not delusional or on drugs."

She was sleep-deprived if the bags under her eyes were any indication, and they'd definitely worked up a sweat together in his cabin. Exhaustion could cause a person to see things that weren't there.

Zane had sense enough to keep that observation to himself.

"I'm frustrated that nothing is being done to figure out what happened to the guy that I found in my room — where his body is, for starters, and maybe, how did he die? There was no blood that I could see, but his face was contorted kind of, like he'd been strangled or at least taken by surprise." She pushed away from him. "Which is why I need your help. I'd like to hire you — "

"Hire me?" Alarm bells went haywire in Zane's head, along with the dawning suspicion that he'd said something he maybe shouldn't have in one of the postcoital chit-chats he always seemed to do after a good orgasm.

"Yes, to investigate what I saw." She rolled her eyes.

Zane sighed. Cammie may not have been drinking all night be he certainly had. "I told you."

"That you're a private investigator?" Cammie looked at him like he'd grown a second head. "Uh, yeah, don't you remember?"

Zane closed his eyes briefly before ushering her to the side and away from potential eavesdroppers. "Listen... I can't help you with this. I have my own" — he cleared his throat then lowered his voice even more — "my own investigation to conduct. I don't have time to follow up on what you think you saw."

"What I *think* I saw?" She crossed her arms and her lips thinned, which, fascinatingly, made her dimples pop. "You don't believe me."

"Cammie, you saw something. I believe that. But maybe it was some guy who'd had one too many and ended up in your cabin somehow."

"You think I tripped over a drunk guy?" She huffed. "You think a drunk guy somehow stumbled into my room, then passed out on my floor with his mouth and eyes open, not breathing, blinking or having a pulse."

When she put it like that... "You *touched* him?"

She threw her hands up. "Of course, I did! I needed to make sure he was dead. I would have performed CPR if I'd thought he had a chance."

"And you told the captain this?" Zane's gut twisted, confirming the *something's so not right* feeling he had when he was speaking with the captain.

"Yes." She crossed her arms again.

Fuck. He really didn't have time to chase two cases in five days. He pinched the bridge of his nose, massaging where he suddenly felt a headache brewing, then closed his eyes.

"Has it occurred to you that your investigation and my dead guy situation might be connected?" Cammie's matter-of-fact tone bypassed his head pain.

He snapped his eyes open but kept his fingers moving against his blooming headache. "I'm working a missing money case."

"And missing money has never led to dead bodies before?" She quirked an eyebrow in such an obvious 'duh' expression that he wanted to laugh. "You can't deny there might be some connection, even a tiny one. By helping me, you might be helping yourself."

She had a point. He lowered his hand. "Fine. Yes, it's possible the two are connected."

"My cabin?" She was already turning, expecting him to follow.

"Your cabin," Zane confirmed with a sigh.

Chapter Three

Cammie probably wouldn't have believed herself if she'd been in Zane's position. A woman, who he'd known for a few hours, claiming that she'd stumbled on a dead body that had somehow gotten up and walked away? Yeah...that screamed straight-up cuckoo. She couldn't totally blame him for not being one hundred percent on board with her theory that his case and the dead guy in her room were connected, either.

"This is very swanky." Zane hadn't moved beyond the door, which meant that Cammie, blocked by his imposing frame, also hadn't stepped inside the room.

"Zane—"

"Hang tight. I just need to look for a minute."

She tried to peek over his shoulder but couldn't— even on tip-toes—get high enough. She attempted to scoot around him, but his torso was as wide and thick as a brick wall. She briefly contemplated bending lower to find a nook or cranny that would give her a view but realized how truly ridiculous that was. *This is my room, dammit!* She slipped her hand around his waist, fanning her fingers low enough to make a suggestion.

He grunted as he finally got the message. "You could have just asked," he chuckled then moved to the side so she could see what he was seeing.

Cammie rolled her eyes but stepped into the space he'd created for her. She wasn't expecting the crush of disappointment that raked through her when she saw that the room looked completely untouched.

Disappointed that there was no dead body?
How morbid.

There wasn't a thing out of place, not even a dent in the carpet. Zane crouched, which seemed like it took some effort, given his height, so she crouched too, trying to see what he was seeing.

Nothing obstructed her view at that level. *Nothing.* Not even a fluff of lint or a speck of dust.

"This carpet isn't plush enough to leave marks." He pushed his hand into the carpet like he was testing its bounce. "The body was where, exactly?"

He stood up, leaving Cammie behind to stare at where she'd last saw the dead man—or thought she'd seen the dead man. *Wouldn't there be some indication that there'd been a body lying right next to my bed?* Blood? A stray hair? Something?

After she'd tripped over the body, then had gotten over the initial shock of finding someone in her room, she had checked his vitals. While his skin hadn't been cold to the touch, it hadn't exactly been warm, either. He'd had no pulse, and he hadn't been breathing. She wasn't an expert on assessing dead bodies, but by the vacant look in the guy's eyes, she was fairly confident that he'd been beyond the point of resuscitation. She'd bolted out of the room in search of help, shouting all the way down the hall until she'd finally found a security guard.

He'd taken her directly to see the captain, promising to send someone to her room to check on the man in her cabin when she'd protested.

Now, looking at the empty space and the virtually untouched room, she had to wonder if she'd really seen what she thought she had.

What if he had been just some drunk guy who had somehow gotten into her room then passed out? *With his eyes open…and no pulse.*

Right. This was not the time for second-guessing. *Chin up, tits out,* as some of the newer the Kitty Cats always said.

She pointed to the spot where the body had lain then started to get up herself.

"Oh, Miss Sheppard! Let me help you!" Ben, her steward, already had his hand under her arm and was heaving her to her feet before she could even glance over her shoulder at him. In the process of helping her stand, he pulled her back a step and the door began to close. She caught Zane's eye seconds before the cabin door swung shut. He gave her a minute shake of his head, so she didn't reach out to stop the door from closing.

"Thank you, Ben." Cammie injected as much bubble into her voice as she could bear and plastered the fakest of fake smiles on her face. "It's been a long night."

"Did you lose something on the floor?" Ben flicked his hair out of his eye. "I can help you look. Was it an earring? I'm a pro at finding missing earrings." He already had his key card out and ready to unlock her door.

It took Cammie more than a few seconds to realize that Ben clearly had no idea what had happened in her room. She put her hand on his to stop him. "Didn't anyone talk to you about the...er...man I found in my room?"

Ben's face blanched. "There was a man in your room? Without your consent?"

Well, yeah, you could say that. "Ben" — she shifted his hand away from the card reader — "I found a dead man in my room. I tripped over him."

His eyes widened to an, almost, comical degree. "A d-d-dead man?" His hand fluttered to his throat. "I-in your room?"

"Nobody came to talk to you? Dilan Ross? Captain Evans? Any of the security team?" She watched his eyes, his face, even his body language, but nothing about Ben screamed duplicity. He seriously had no idea what she was talking about.

"No! I made my rounds at midnight like I always do. I came in to your room to turn down your covers like I do in every room on my decks, but then I went to bed. I left a few extra chocolates on your pillow." He wrung his hands. "I'm so sorry, Miss Sheppard. I can't imagine what you must be going through. A dead man in your room! I have to tell someone — "

He was so sweet and earnest that Cammie wanted to give him a hug and tell him it was all going to be okay. "I've already notified security and the captain."

Ben frowned. "Why aren't they here?"

Good question.

"Not that I'd question the decisions of...well...I mean, I'm not a qualified to make judgments..." He seemed to be choking on his words as he backpedaled from his initial reaction. "I'm sure the captain and Chief Ross know what they're doing, though. I wouldn't want them to think that I would question — "

Poor soul.

"It's okay, Ben." She squeezed his arm in an attempt to reassure him. "What brought you up here now?"

Ben lost some of his spooked expression as his brain seemed to click to work mode. "It's five-thirty. My shift starts at five. I like to be up here for the early risers."

It's five-thirty? Cammie closed her eyes briefly. She'd been running on adrenaline all night.

"Is the body still in there?" Ben had his key card out again.

Cammie sighed. "The body is gone." She rubbed her eyes. "When I alerted security and they came here to check, the body had disappeared." *Somehow.*

Ben's face went through a sliding scale of 'what the fuck'. His mouth twitched but no words came out. The door swung open.

"You two get locked out?" Zane said as he met her eyes again. She didn't need his words to know that he'd found nothing.

Ben scanned the room, looking every which way before landing on Zane. "Did you find anything?"

"You're the steward for this deck?" Zane ignored Ben's question and speared him with what could only be descripted as an interrogative stare.

"This is Ben," Cammie said as she tried to soften Zane's approach. She knew he didn't want people to know he was a PI, but right now he was coming off as full-on detective. It made her wonder what had brought him to this chapter of his life. Had he been a police officer before? There was something very commanding about him. "He last checked my room at midnight then went to bed."

Zane scrutinized Ben in a way that made Cammie want to squirm.

"Tell me, Ben. Hypothetically speaking, if a body were to be shoved overboard..." He motioned to the balcony.

Ben's eyes bugged out. "Over the balcony?" He shook his head. "Impossible. We'd know if someone went overboard. There are sensors—"

He started to walk into the room, but Zane got in his way. "That's what I thought." He held his hand out to Cammie. "Everything seems fine in here now."

Cammie took his hand cautiously, wondering if he was implying that she hadn't seen what she thought she'd seen.

"You're clearly exhausted, Cammie. I think it would be good if you got some sleep," Zane added, which seemed to take him out of detective mode and straight into concerned friend mode.

Cammie felt his words and attitude shift like a blow to the chest. She locked eyes with him, searching for his truth. All she saw was worry and compassion, and it made her want to cry and scream at the same time. *He doesn't believe me. There's no evidence.* It was her word against...what? A missing dead man?

She'd never felt so defeated in her life.

"Yes, that's probably a good idea." Ben latched onto Zane's words. "You look exhausted, Miss Sheppard. I can get you a nice chamomile..."

"No, thank you, Ben," Cammie croaked. Her shoulders slumped, the weight of her defeat like an anchor...or maybe a noose. She was suddenly too tired to argue. Four people believed she was lying.

"We're fine here, Ben." Zane used his bulk again to move Ben toward the door. "I've promised Captain Evans that I'll take care of Cammie." He lowered his voice but not enough so Cammie couldn't hear. "I'll keep an eye on her."

Ben's eyes widened and he nodded. "Very good, okay." He craned his neck to look over Zane's shoulder. "Call me if you need anything, Miss Sheppard."

She turned her back on both of them, fighting against her warring emotions. She wanted to punch something. She wanted to crumple into a heap on her bed and sob.

The door whooshed shut.

"Grab your stuff."

Cammie snapped out of her head and frowned over her shoulder at Zane. He was already headed into her closet. "We can always come back for more clothes. You don't want to take too much. Make it look like you're staying here." He motioned to the bed. "Mess up the sheets a bit."

"What?" His pivot wasn't registering, and she just stared after him like the empty space around her would fill in the blanks somehow.

He poked his head out of the closet. "Obviously you can't stay here. I mean, unless you're okay with sleeping next to a ghost...and knowing what you know?"

Her stomach fluttered and the weight on her shoulders lifted. "You believe me?"

He gave her a 'yeah, duh' look before disappearing into the closet again.

Even without evidence, Zane believed her.

Okay then.

The investigation was still on. No evidence? No problem! She was Cammie Sheppard. She'd find a way to prove what happened and figure out what the hell was going on.

She scanned the room, then beelined for the blinds. One flick of a button and they slowly started to drop. Better if Ben thought she slept the morning away when he came in later to clean or whatever it was he did on his shift.

Zane came out of her closet with a pair of jogging pants and a T-shirt. "These okay for sleeping?"

Cammie wanted to laugh. *No, not really.* She usually slept naked, but she was assuming she was headed to Zane's room and, despite their earlier intimacy, didn't want to make things weird. "Yep. Great, thanks."

She yanked the folded-down comforter nearly off the bed then mussed up the sheets. Zane came around the other side and swiped the chocolates off before punching the pillows a few times, making it look like a head had rested there.

Cammie detoured to the bathroom to collect the toiletries she'd need, then grabbed a few other things from the closet. Zane had shoved her comfortable clothes into a clean laundry bag, so she added the extra things she'd collected.

"Ready?" He unwrapped one of the chocolates then popped it into his mouth.

"We are headed to your room, right?" She waved away the wrapped chocolate he held out for her.

"Yeah, I'll take the floor. Eventually." He opened that chocolate, too, then ate it. "We've got some things to do first."

For a split-second Cammie had the most ludicrous thought race through her mind — *Sex? Now? Hell yes!*

Sure, she could absolutely use a good fucking, maybe some more bondage play —

"I've got access to the traveler manifest. It has details that might help us find the dead guy."

Ohhhhh, right. Cammie's cheeks heated. *Oopsie…not thinking of sex….*

"You okay?" He paused with his hand on the door.

She waved him off. "Yeah, yeah, lead the way." She bypassed the place where the body had been.

"We can order some room service, get some caffeine and food." He held the door open.

"Good plan," she said as she swept past him.

Sex. Sheesh! Can someone say 'gutter brain'?

C h a p t e r   F o u r

The lack of evidence pointed to...well, not good things, as far as Zane was concerned. Seeing the absolute dejection on Cammie's face and posture had firmed up his resolve to get to the bottom of things for her. Even though there was no body and no obvious disturbance in her room, it wasn't all without hope.

Cammie was using the restroom and not currently looking over his shoulder, so Zane checked the security cameras he had access to. He wasn't sure what he'd see, so he thought it might be better to check the feeds without Cammie around.

It hadn't taken him long to hack into the cruise ship's databases, which was something else he'd have to report to Dark Matter's CEO. Zane wasn't trained as a computer geek. He'd just kind of picked things up here and there, but if it only took him twenty minutes to get in and have access to all kinds of personal information, the company needed to know about the potential security risk.

A few clicks and he'd zeroed in on Cammie's deck and the feed was dead. *Wonderful.* There was no video evidence and no way of knowing who might have entered then exited Cammie's room. Very suspicious, especially considering that Chief Ross had said he'd checked the camera feed from Cammie's deck. Obviously, that was a lie. Several of the decks didn't seem to have security cameras — or at least they weren't currently working. Shoddy surveillance? Or something else?

He'd have to figure out a way to dig into that with the Chief of Security, because it definitely screamed something nefarious and the man had obviously not spoken to Ben the steward like he'd told the captain he had. It was clear that Ben had no idea what was going on — or, at least, he hadn't been filled in completely. So, the Chief of Security was hiding something or he was incompetent. Maybe a bit of both.

He added that to his mental list of things to investigate.

For now…Zane flipped to the traveler manifest.

"You said he had dark hair, blue eyes?" Zane clicked a few commands to narrow down his search. There were fifteen hundred souls on board the Dark Matter Fetish Cruise, and none of them had been required to give a photo. Each traveler was documented with height, weight, age and description, but only a few had a picture to go along with their files. Zane assumed there was a certain level of anonymity granted them, due to the nature of the cruise being kink and all, but as far as security went, it was another roadblock to finding answers for Cammie. "Thirties?"

Cammie maneuvered in the tight space then flopped on the bed next to him. She smelled like mint and apples. Her face was clean of makeup—not that she wore very much—and it gave her a younger, more innocent look that revved Zane's Dom side to attention. "Maybe twenties, I think."

They'd eaten their fill of room service breakfast and had downed an entire carafe of coffee between the two of them. She'd put on her jogging suit and looked as cozy as he'd hoped when he'd picked that outfit. He wanted to rip her clothes off, tie her up then fuck her silly. He also wanted to curl up with her and take a nap. He was exhausted and, by the dazed look in her eyes, so was she. Sex would have to wait.

He typed the age range into his query then started the algorithm. "This might take a minute."

Cammie yawned. Zane stretched his back and groaned as his spine cracked.

"You don't have to sleep on the floor." Her words were punctuated by a giant yawn that made her dimples pop when she closed her mouth.

Her sexy little mouth that had taken his cock so prettily hours before was just begging for a kiss.

"I don't want to make you uncomfortable." He reordered his priorities. They would sleep then fuck then get on with the job, because even though Cammie had a mystery of her own, Zane was on the clock with his own investigation and, so far, he had zero leads.

Of course, that all depended on whether Cammie wanted to fuck him again. Dead bodies kind of had a kill-joy effect on fun and games.

"After what we did earlier?" Cammie snorted. "I think we're well past the point of worrying about things like that. Besides, I'm not quite finished with you." She nudged him with her shoulder. "And I think you're not quite done with me, either."

"Hell no, I'm not." Zane grinned and his cock shot through with heat. "If you're sure…after everything that's happened."

"I'm a big girl." Cammie touched his arm. "And I'm not made of glass. But I am exhausted, so maybe after a few hours' sleep?"

Zane yawned too, couldn't help himself. He was depleted, ready to get a few hours of shut-eye, at least, no matter what his dick was demanding. "Good plan." He checked the progress of the program. "This is taking longer than I thought it would." He set the computer on the bedside table.

"Leave it for now." Cammie tugged him down then curled herself up in a blanket like a snug little burrito.

He wasn't going to lie. It felt good to be nestled next to a beauty like Cammie. Not just because it was a warm body for his cold heart but because it meant — for a little while anyway — that he didn't have to be alone with himself, and that truly did make this feel like a vacation.

* * * *

Zane was having the best dream. His dick, hard and weeping, was being stroked by a firm grip. Warm, soft kisses trailed along his jaw, and he swore he felt the cushioned press of tits on his chest.

"Zane," Cammie's chocolate-coated voice whispered into his dream, "time to wake up."

He slowly opened his eyes.

Cammie hovered over him, her huge tits bare, her dark nipples peaked and begging for his mouth. "I need you," she purred as she nipped at his jaw.

He growled as he came fully awake. "I thought I was dreaming." She'd already worked his boxers down his legs, so he kicked them off.

Cammie laughed in her husky way before licking down his neck, over his collarbone then across his pec. She circled one nipple, then the other, flicking and teasing and forcing him to repay the favor. He cupped her breasts, loving how they filled his hands, then thumbed her nipples.

She wiggled herself away, obviously intent on making her way to his cock, but he had other plans.

"Flip around," he ordered, and Cammie immediately did as she was told.

With her pussy hovering above his face, Cammie got to work on his dick, slurping and sucking her way down until she suctioned her lips around his base. Her mouth was glorious, but her pussy was even better. He spread her legs then eased her down so her sweet cunt was within his tongue's reach. He licked her from clit to asshole, circling her puckered hole a few times before returning to her clit. He delved into her pussy with his tongue, probing her, savoring her taste, swallowing her juice. This was the best way to wake up, with pussy juice slipping along his tongue and a sexy woman sucking his cock. *Pure bliss.*

She used one hand to massage his balls as she pumped his cock in a steady rhythm. He slipped two fingers into her hole in search of the little nub that would make her squirt, all the while flicking her clit to the same tempo as her blow job.

She sucked on his balls then licked her way up to his tip, tonguing against his most sensitive spot, just under the ridge of his crown. He writhed and moaned but didn't unlatch from her clit, sucking a little harder, making her squirm.

He loved her little moans and the way she swayed her body as her orgasm began to crest. They'd only been intimate a few times, but Zane already knew Cammie's tells — the way her breath hitched, how her legs quivered and her toes curled, the way she shuddered and groaned then finally exploded, squirting juice all over his face, coating him, making his dick as hard as rock.

Her climax pulled the trigger on his, and he groaned through another atomic bomb as cum spewed into Cammie's mouth. It went on forever, spurting jets down Cammie's throat, wringing him out, making him collapse back at the same time that Cammie flopped to the side and lay, like him, nearly comatose.

There was a quick knock. "Housekeeping!" Then the beep of the card reader.

"Wait!" Cammie bolted off the bed, scrambling to hold one hand against the door and the other on the door handle, which had already begun to move. "Can you come back later?"

"Yes, of course!" a muffled voice said. The door handle snapped back to place. "I'll clean the room next door first."

Cammie leaned against the door with a whoosh of breath. "That would have been awkward."

"I'm sure he's seen worse." Zane laughed. "Poor guy."

Cammie nodded, one hand at her brow, then she burst into a fit of giggles that made Zane's stomach bubble in a weird way. He couldn't help it. He busted out laughing, too, and couldn't seem to stop, not when Cammie started snorting in the most unexpectedly adorable way. She had tears streaming over her face and her dimples looked ready to explode out of her cheeks. She flopped on the bed, curled up into a ball and continued to giggle.

It had been a long time since he'd had such fun with anyone, laughing so hard that his stomach hurt? Yeah, that had happened…well, maybe *never* in his life. He clasped Cammie's hand then brought it to his lips for a kiss. "Thank you."

A few more giggles erupted from her before she could manage words. "What for?"

He shrugged then kissed her hand again. *For chasing away the shadows*, he wanted to say but that was too heavy for a cruise fling and not something he wanted to get into, anyway.

They lay there, hand-in-hand, for another few minutes, their breathing charged. Zane's heart beat at hyper speed, so much adrenaline coursing through his body that he felt like he could go for a run…if he did that kind of thing, which he didn't, not anymore.

The sound of a vacuum cleaner next door reminded him that they had limited time to get up and out of his cabin.

"I guess we should get on with the day." Zane sat up then grabbed his laptop. The algorithm had done its job. "There are four hits." Four out of fifteen hundred needles in one giant haystack.

Cammie leaned in to get a better look. "What's the plan?"

"Process of elimination. We hunt these guys down, and whoever's missing is our dead man." He made it sound easy, but in truth, searching out these guys, none of whom had pictures, would be a nightmare and a time suck. Zane could only hope that he'd find a way to dig into his own investigation along the way.

Cammie nodded. "I'm going to head back to my room so I can shower and grab some fresh clothes." She started to shift off the bed.

Zane wanted to stop her. He wanted to say 'fuck it', put the 'do not disturb' sign on his door and stay in bed all day with Cammie. Instead, he watched her root around for her discarded clothes.

"Meet you on the Sky Deck in forty-five?" She slipped on her pants, no panties, which he found super intriguing, then grabbed her shirt.

Zane shook his head as he tapped the screen. "Not the Sky Deck. The itinerary today is packed with activities. Let's meet in the atrium and see if we can find some kind of attendance list."

"Good plan." She put her hand on the door, ready to breeze out of his world once again.

"Cammie, wait."

She paused, one eyebrow hitched, but he didn't give her a chance to ask why, because he was already off the bed and crowding her. He bullied her back until she had nowhere left to go. "Wear a dress like the one you had on when we met."

She was looking him dead in the eyes as she bit her bottom lip then nodded. "Yes, Sir."

Oh shit, this woman! His cock, hard all over again, demanded that he fuck her right up against the door, but he reined himself in. He cupped her face then kissed her. It wasn't a punishing kiss or a demanding one. He kept it soft and teasing, stroking her with a lazy slowness that made her breath come quick and her body quiver against his.

He pulled back, satisfied when she sighed. "No panties."

The glint in Cammie's eyes made him realize that she'd had no intention of wearing panties anyway. "Yes, Sir."

Fuck, he loved the sound of that.

Chapter Five

Cammie spotted Zane before he spotted her. He was wearing brown khaki shorts and a blue button-up short-sleeved shirt. As he stepped into the atrium, he scanned the crowd, eyes widening as he took it all in. There was so much to look at. Cammie had gorged herself endlessly when she'd first arrived. Not only were the woman dressed in latex and fishnet that showcased all their assets but so were the men. There was a lot of skin showing and very little left to the imagination — totally sexy. The crew were serving drinks and snacks as well as directing people this way and that toward the many booths where vendors had set up their fetish wares.

Cammie had put on a simple white halter tank that displayed her ample cleavage marvelously and a wispy black skirt that she could twirl high enough to show off her bare-naked ass if she wanted.

Zane accepted a flute of champagne from one of the servers then took a swig as he continued to hunt her down.

Cammie's breath hitched when his gaze found her. She gasped a little when his eyes locked in, giving her a hungry once-over that made her knees wobble.

This man was accelerant to her flame. Her body melted on the spot as he walked toward her, looking like a man full of octane. The crowd parted on instinct, and Cammie couldn't help but burn a little more because he was so commanding and in charge.

"Love that dress." His gruff voice sent shivers over her skin.

"It's a skirt, actually." The sass just slipped out and Zane growled in response. He curled his arm around her waist and hoisted her against his body.

"I don't care what it is." He reached under her skirt to cup her pussy with his free hand, jolting her, making her squirm as he slipped a couple of fingers into her hole.

She choked on a moan. Her body revved up, ready to spontaneously combust. Anyone could see what he was doing, and yet no one was paying any attention — or at least, no one *appeared* to be paying attention. She wondered just how far they could go without anyone noticing…or caring. She hoisted herself up his body, her arms around his neck, fingers digging into the short stubble at the base of his skull.

"I found Steven Posh," he said against her ear, as if he was whispering dirty talk instead of some guy's name.

"Huh?" She was so consumed by his fingers stroking her pussy and his thumb rubbing her clit that coherent thought was not within her reach.

"Our first guy, Steven Posh. He's a vendor, selling vibrators over there — at the booth with all the lights." He maintained his grip on her waist so she couldn't move more than a slight shift backward, enough to look up at Zane. He pulled his hand out from under her skirt then slipped his fingers into his mouth, his eyes locked with hers as he licked her juice. It was the hottest thing she'd ever seen, like he was savoring her lust. Her body twisted and curled, aching for another round with Zane, right here, right now — audience be damned.

His words finally caught up to her, though, and, somehow, she managed to turn her head enough to see what Zane was talking about. The booth with the vibrators was a popular one, and the guy selling dildos and various other phallic devices was a pretty good likeness of the guy she'd found on her floor — except it wasn't him. His jaw was all wrong — round instead of angular — and his eyes were vividly green. His hair was curly and long as well, definitely more model material than the dead man had been. Not that he hadn't been attractive… The dead man…ugh…hadn't been ugly… only grotesquely dead. *Why am I so worried about hurting a dead man's feelings?*

"Hello, you two!" A stunning brunette swept up to them, her green eyes bright and smile one-hundred-percent fake. "My name is Sherri Bolt." She looked at them full of expectation, nodding in a way that suggested it was their turn to speak.

Zane let Cammie slide back to the floor and released his grip on her waist. Luckily her skirt didn't ride up as she went down or she'd be putting on a show of her own for the crowd.

"Cammie Sheppard." Cammie had enough experience event planning to know that this lady was one of the event managers. Her demeanor screamed 'woman in charge'. She was definitely on a mission to recruit more people into whatever was in play for the day. "And this is Zane Roberts."

"Did you two *come* together?" The way she said 'come' made Cammie think that Sherri had seen exactly what they'd been up to moments before, and that made Cammie's face burn red hot. "Or did you find one another on board?"

"Oh, we've *come* together many times, Sherri." Zane winked before adding, "If you don't mind, Cammie is eager to check out the other vendors."

Cammie wanted to die, seriously. Did he just say that? Out loud? Oblivious to her embarrassment, Zane cupped her ass and gave her a squeeze that made her gasp.

"Of course, yes. Don't let me hold you up." Sherri's knowing eyes sparked as she looked from Zane to Cammie. "Wouldn't want to get in the way of your fun. Just remember that there's a series of workshops this afternoon and" — she tapped away on her iPad — "yes, just as I thought, neither of you are signed up for anything."

"We'll catch up with you later about that, Sherri," Cammie said as she tugged Zane away.

"What my woman wants, my woman gets," Zane said over his shoulder as he let Cammie pull him farther into the crowd.

"What was that?" She was both mortified and turned on by Zane's over-the-top TMI with Sherri. "Did you really have to make a 'come' joke?"

"Yes, if we want the crew believing that we're enjoying the cruise." Zane stopped her by pulling her into his arms. "Look behind us."

Angela Addams

Cammie did as he said and found herself staring at Chief Ross in all his imposing glory *and* he was staring back. So, they were being watched. *Wonderful.*

"I thought it would be wise to play a part. I've heard some of the other men saying more pervy things and getting away with it." He shifted her sideways so his arm draped over her shoulder. "I'm sorry if I embarrassed you."

"I wasn't embarrassed," she lied. "More shocked." Now that she understood where he was coming from, she actually thought his acting was quite impressive, believable and wise. If they had a cover, then no one would suspect that they were up to something. "It might have been a good idea to discuss strategy before we got started."

"I'm more a fly-by-the-seat-of-my-pants kind of guy." Zane laughed. "Besides, Sherri started it."

Cammie found the idea of zero planning appalling and also intriguing. She didn't really know a thing about Zane, his success or his methods, but he had to have some kind of reputation as a PI if Dark Matter Inc. had hired him. The CEO, Cal Underwood, was an exacting man who was as into perfection as her own boss, Sabine Cowan, but he stretched himself a little too thin with his variety of moneymaking schemes. Since they flirted with similar circles of clientele, Cammie was very familiar with Cal and his opinion of people. If he'd hired Zane to look into problems on his cruise line, he knew and expected that Zane would deliver, which meant that Zane had to be good.

Cammie grinned up at him. "All right, perv, you do you." A little spontaneity wouldn't kill her. "But sooner or later we're going to have to go to one of the events Sherri talked about. Better for us to choose and have a

51

bit of preplanning rather than having someone else slot us in to something."

"Good point." He whipped out his phone, his grin fully engaged, tapped a few times then turned the screen to face her.

Role Play –Expert Level
Cammie Sheppard
Enrolled
Zane Roberts
Enrolled

"You signed us up for a workshop?" She wanted to eat her words from seconds before. *"You do you."* Ugh. She hadn't meant for Zane to sign them up right away!

She'd never really experienced role play and had always kind of thought it was more of a couples thing to do...like a long-term couple, two or more people who had a relationship that would extend over time to include some kind of role playing. For the last few years, all Cammie had given herself time to do was indulge in hook-ups, probably because a deeper level of intimacy and vulnerability gave her hives and cut into her productivity.

"I thought it looked interesting." His grin faltered as he registered her expression. "No pressure. It's just something to get Sherri off our backs. We don't have to go."

"No, it's a smart idea." She forced those words out, even though her stomach clenched down on the jangle of nerves rattling inside her.

"Obviously Steven Posh isn't our guy." Zane tugged her forward, breaking the weirdly awkward moment with a snap. "But I have a lead on where to find our next target, Ed Fulton."

* * * *

The casino was full of people, and they were all glued to one game or another. There was no way Cammie and Zane would be able to carry on a covert conversation with all the dinging, ticking, beeping and bells going off around them. Zane used a series of hand gestures to indicate that they needed to go over to the card tables, which were located, apparently, at the back of the casino, then he mouthed what Cammie thought was Blackjack.

Zane took her hand, entwining his thick fingers with hers, then guided her in a curvy, roundabout way through the gamblers. Cammie had never really gotten the point of gambling, especially knowing that the house inevitably won. She wasn't the type to get caught up in the excitement of hoping for a big win, because she knew the odds weren't in her favor. But winding her way through the crowd gave her an appreciation of just how much adrenaline was pumping through each gambler's veins. Even though she wasn't an adrenaline junkie, she could appreciate the allure of hitting the button or throwing the dice and taking a chance on luck. If the ruddy cheeks, dilated pupils, loud peals of laughter and heart-stopping gasps were any indication, the casino was one of the most intoxicating places to be. She could well imagine how much sexual tension could exist just under the surface of things.

They got to the Blackjack table and the white noise dropped off, almost like they'd passed through a sound barrier of some sort. There was soft music playing and some conversation, but otherwise, it was missing all the hoopla from a few feet away.

"I don't see him but that doesn't mean he isn't here. According to my research, he's a high roller." Zane tugged her toward one of the tables. "Let's play a few rounds and wait."

She dug in her heels on impulse. She had no desire to throw money away, then remembered that she was playing a part. She needed to go along with the subterfuge, just in case Chief Ross had followed them into the casino.

If Zane noticed her hesitation, he didn't say anything. Instead, he guided her to a table, leaned in and whispered, "I'll play. You be my good luck charm. Security has many eyes in here." Then he kissed her forehead in the most endearing way that left Cammie unable to do much more than nod.

She had to give him credit. He was damn observant if he already knew what she'd be comfortable with. She glanced up briefly to note the dozen or so opaque domes overhead. Of course, there'd be cameras in this space—whether or not they worked was another thing altogether. All the same, this was yet another opportunity for Cammie and Zane to present as a normal couple doing normal couple things.

She waited until Zane had settled himself on his stool then draped her arm over his shoulder.

While the slots had been a relatively equal mix of men and woman, the card tables were occupied almost exclusively by men. There were female servers, dressed in gorgeous black lace cocktail dresses and stiletto heels, buzzing in and out, dropping off drinks and taking new orders. Men slipped hundred-dollar chips onto their trays as they wove through the crowd, which seemed generous, but also, to Cammie's horror, came with strings attached. A pat on the ass here, a stray hand caressing a breast there, as if these ladies had signed up to manhandled just because they were dressed as they were.

Even though she worked in the sex industry, it always shocked her when anyone assumed that the way a woman dressed was consent for touching. It *never* was.

Zane had only been playing for a handful of minutes before Cammie realized that this was not a game purely of chance. Zane had to be counting cards in some capacity because he truly had skill at knowing when to hit or stand. He was already up a few hundred dollars when Cammie spotted Ed Fulton.

He was a little older than the last guy, maybe still in his twenties. His face was youthful looking, but he was balding, which aged him upon first glimpse. It made Cammie wonder if she had the right guy after all. She'd have to get a closer look.

She leaned in to Zane, whispering against his ear, "I think I found him. Two tables over, second seat. I'm going to confirm."

She didn't wait for Zane to acknowledge he'd heard her and was already at the table before she gave much thought to how she'd confirm anything.

"Oh, look who it is!" Bill Haversmith was seated at the same table and he practically jumped out of his chair to greet her. "My little beauty, Cammie! I knew you were a vixen, gambling with the big boys, eh? Well, here, take my seat. I want to see what you can do!"

Fuuuuck! She hadn't seen Bill sitting there. What a tragic mistake.

Cammie was trapped, and her damn feet didn't get the memo to turn the other way and run. Instead, she continued right into Bill's web so he could usher her into his vacated seat.

"Come on, Eddie. Make room, make room!" Bill shouted at the man sitting next to Cammie, so he could wedge himself somewhat between them.

Cammie gave Eddie a winced smile and mouthed 'sorry', but he didn't seem to care. At least she had confirmation that the guy sitting next to her was Ed Fulton and that he was very much alive. *Two down, two to go.*

"I'm going to spot darling Cammie her first bet." Bill slid a five-thousand-dollar chip from his pile.

Cammie sputtered over the amount, choking on her heart as it tried to hammer its way out of her mouth.

"Now, don't you argue, my pet. I'm forcing you to be here, so let's see if you're as lucky as I think you are." Bill put a heavy hand on her shoulder.

Cammie squirmed, her body desperate for flight, but she grounded herself on the stool, forcing herself to stay put. She didn't want to create a scene by running out of the casino full tilt in order to get away from Bill's attention. The guy irritated her like nothing else, especially since she really, really didn't want to waste her time gambling, even with someone else's money.

She'd only watched Zane for a few minutes, and yes, she understood the concept of Blackjack, but she was no risk taker. Every time Zane had hit, her gut feeling had been to stand, even if the cards were low.

She wiped her hands on her skirt. There was no getting out of this now, not if she was committed to her investigation — which she was.

She forced a smile then placed her bet.

Chapter Six

Zane stood back and watched Cammie slide her whopping five-thousand-dollar chip forward. He had no idea that she was such a risk taker. In fact, everything he'd seen so far kind of made him think that she didn't like high stakes. It gave him a little high seeing how her hands shook, just a slight vibration, not that he could blame her. It was a lot of money to possibly lose.

The dealer slid the cards out for each player then flipped them. They were all low numbers, including hers—three of hearts and five of spades. The dealer's showing card was a Jack. Zane would hit without a second thought, but Cammie liked to plan, and despite being a wonderful sub, she liked to be in control. Blackjack had an element of luck, for sure. A player couldn't control what cards the dealer dealt, but it was possible, with a careful eye, to make a strategic move.

Each player ahead of Cammie hit then stayed. The dealer hovered, waiting for her to indicate what she wanted. She tapped the table. *Hit.* Zane let his breath slide out slowly, hoping for a good card to come Cammie's way. Five thousand dollars was a lot to hand over in one go.

The dealer slid her card out, flipped it, Ace of spades.

She slashed her hand over the cards. *Stay.*

Cammie's shoulders were scrunched almost to her ears. Zane moved forward, ready to ease his hands over those tense muscles when the big guy standing next to her leaned in and whisper-shouted at her, "That's my girl. You've got him now!"

His *girl? What the fuck?*

The dealer flipped his hidden card. Two of Clubs. He hit again, Queen of Hearts. Twenty-Two. Cammie won!

She sat there like a statue while the big guy cheered. "You doubled your money, sweetheart!"

"It's your money," she said as she started to stand.

"Don't be silly now! You won it fair and square." He put his hand on her shoulder to keep her from getting up. "You're not going to leave, are you, honey? You're just getting started! Now you've got your own money to bet with."

"Thank you, Mr. Haversmith, but I really need to find—"

"Cammie, there you are." Taking the cue, Zane moved in to help her from her seat and away from Bill Haversmith's meaty hand. Zane knew the man by name only. *Millionaire. Womanizer. Supposedly camera-phobic or at least so elusive that there were no actual pictures of the guy.* He was the number one person of interest in Zane's investigation. Haversmith had been one of few travelers to make repeats trips on Dark Matter cruise ships in the last six months. Five out of six, in fact.

Bill took Zane in with a narrowed glare. He even puffed his chest out like he was actually thinking he could take Zane on—as if the man seriously thought Cammie would appreciate being fought over.

"Mr. Haversmith, this is my good friend, Zane Roberts." Cammie slid herself against Zane's side, and he draped his arm over her shoulder to nestle her in closer.

"Well, good to meet you, son," Bill said, his hand out to shake.

Zane bristled at the patronizing tone, but he refused to rise to the bait. "Good to meet you too, sir." They shook hands and, in a classic power move, Bill squeezed just a little too tightly. "Are you the Bill Haversmith who owns Zenith Industries?"

"That I am! The one and only." Bill puffed his chest out even more as his eyes slid to Cammie briefly before returning to Zane's.

"You have a very impressive portfolio."

Bill narrowed his eyes again. "That I do… Say…you wouldn't happen to be an investment banker, would ya?"

"You got me, Bill!" Zane laughed in his own patronizing way. "Maybe we could get a drink and talk—"

"I'm afraid that's not the kind of trip I'm on, Zane." Bill winked. "But you can call my office any time to schedule a meeting." He slipped a business card out of his pocket and handed it to Zane.

"Thank you, sir, I will." Zane squeezed Cammie's shoulder. "And you're right… We're not on that kind of trip, either, are we, Cammie?"

"It was really fun playing a round of cards, Mr. Haversmith." Cammie started to turn, pulling Zane with her.

"Hey now, my dear, you're not leaving yet."

Cammie tensed and Zane flashed a glare toward Bill, but he wasn't looking at Zane. His eyes were locked on Cammie, along with a smarmy smile and his outstretched hand.

"You can't leave without your winnings." He handed her a five-thousand-dollar chip.

"I couldn't!" Cammie said, her cheeks flushing.

"I insist. Treat yourselves to a top-tier spa afternoon." He forced the chip into her hand. "I hear they have some of the rarest mud on board."

Did he say 'mud'?

Haversmith winked at Cammie. "Gets into all the crevasses and creases, if you know what I mean."

"I've heard good things about mud baths." Cammie maintained eye contact with Haversmith, a saccharine smile plastered on her face, the clearest 'fuck you' Zane had ever seen. "Thank you, Mr. Haversmith, you're very generous."

"Psh! What's five grand?" He grinned. "You kids have fun."

So patronizing.

"We certainly will!" Cammie clenched the chip, holding it up like a prize before turning with Zane toward the exit.

To anyone watching, it would look like Zane was leading Cammie out of the card room, but she was the one with a death grip on his hand that was draped over her shoulder, tugging him to keep up with her quick steps.

The smile was gone from her lips and her eyes darted this way and that as she scanned the area ahead of them.

Apparently spotting what she was looking for, Cammie steered them to the side then dropped the five-thousand-dollar chip onto a passing waitress's tray. The waitress didn't even notice. That's how smooth Cammie was.

Now, that's how to make a statement.

Zane's chest filled with pride that Cammie would so casually discard that much gifted money from a man like Haversmith. The millionaire was definitely the sort of guy who thought he owned people and bought his way into and out of situations to his liking. Cammie was clearly the sort of woman who couldn't be bought.

"Thanks for the rescue," Cammie said without disentangling herself from Zane as they made their way out of the casino and through the atrium once again. "You hungry? I'm famished. Let's check out the food."

There were a lot of dining choices on board the cruise, aside from the main dining hall where most of the more formal lunches and dinners happened. Cammie guided them to a smoked meat bistro that had caught Zane's eye already, and he marveled at Cammie's ability to read his mind and his stomach. The bistro had one table for two left.

Meant to be.

"I'm a huge fan of smoked ribs," she said with a wide grin. "I could eat my weight in pork when it's done right."

Zane patted his belly. "I'm with you there. I could eat my weight in most kinds of meat, if I'm going to be honest." Zane was the first to admit that his love of food exceeded his love of exercise. He had a cushion on his body that he could probably starve away, but he'd never been one for diets. He usually kept up an intense interval workout schedule so that he could eat the way he liked, but over the last year he'd slacked a bit—*a lot*. One too many late-night stakeouts in his car with only fast food as his company and no workouts for months.

Cammie laughed in a knowing way. "I do enjoy big men with healthy appetites."

"Lucky me." Zane winked. He'd always been drawn to bigger woman as well, and Cammie, with all her curves, fit the bill perfectly. The fact that she was enthusiastic about smoked meat only made her that much more appealing. "So, how do you know Haversmith?"

Cammie rolled her eyes. "I was scouting some men for work and had the pleasure of meeting Bill during the mixer. Actually, just before I met you."

"Scouting men for work, eh? Sounds naughty." Zane already knew that Cammie worked for Cowan Enterprises as a personal assistant to the CEO Sabine Cowan, and he knew that her boss's business was rooted in the sex industry. He didn't need a background check to get that information. Everyone, every *man*, knew who the Kitty Cats were, and Zane was intimately familiar with several of the Kitty Cat clubs in New York.

"Not like that," she laughed. "We have a Gentlemen's Club for...well...stinking rich men. Haversmith seemed like a good candidate."

"Oh yeah, I'd say. The man does love women." *And money. And exploiting women with his money.* In the research Zane had already done, Bill Haversmith had quite a few scandals come his way over the years, all which had involved female staff who'd claimed mistreatment, sexual harassment and bullying — that kind of thing. All allegations were never proven and seemed to just disappear, never to be spoken of again. Zane would bet they'd been bought off, likely intimidated into staying quiet. "He has a reputation for being a pig. Not sure that's what you want in your Gentlemen's Club."

"Our security team always does a thorough background check before we let anyone buy into the club, but thanks for the tip." They both knew she'd already experienced Haversmith's pushiness. "If we did let him in, it would be at a premium price, but really I'd like to erase Bill from my memory completely if I could."

"Are you two ready to order?" The waiter popped up next to them like a specter out of thin air.

Cammie jolted and gasped. "Oh gosh, you startled me!"

Zane found her jumpiness to be endearing, which made him pause. He wasn't one to seek out the company of others and yet he found spending time with Cammie was quickly becoming one of his favorite things to do.

"I'm ready. You?" Cammie plucked him out of his head with a snap of their shared menu.

"Hell yes." Zane pointed at the menu then paused. "You have a notepad? This is going to be a big order."

They both ordered more food than they would probably finish, but everything sounded so enticing that Zane couldn't help himself — and apparently neither could Cammie. He appreciated a woman who could eat him under the table. It actually had felt like a kindred soul moment when Cammie had rattled off the list of meat as well as an impressive amount of carbs she wanted to try.

"Tell me something that no one really knows about you that might surprise me." Cammie's eyes sparkled mischievously.

Right away Zane's thoughts turned dark—dipping straight into his murky past. "Oh…that's a tough one." He motioned her way. "You go first."

"That's not how this game goes." Cammie pouted and her dimples popped. "It doesn't have to be something major—like maybe you're the kind of guy who likes watching romance movies more than action."

"Doesn't every guy have a secret romance addiction?"

Cammie laughed. "I wish."

"Okay, I have a soft spot for rescue animals, and any time I see one of those sad puppy ads for donating money, I always pay up." Which was true. He was a total sucker for helping animals. They didn't deserve the horrid treatment they sometimes endured.

"Ahhh, that's so sweet." Cammie touched his hand briefly but he turned his palm up and coaxed her to keep her hand there.

"Your turn. Tell me something people would be surprised to learn about you." He rubbed his thumb over the back of her hand. This was for appearances only—never knew who was watching. That's what he was telling himself, anyway. It had nothing to do with how nice it felt to get close to someone like Cammie, even for a few minutes.

"I'm a brown belt in Jujitsu." Cammie beamed. "I love that no one would look at me and think that."

"I'm impressed," Zane said. While he hadn't trained in any one martial art himself, he knew that being proficient in any discipline wasn't really about how you looked physically as much as it was about how skilled you were. While a lot of meathead guys he knew in his past had been focused on their physique, being ripped and looking like a badass, most of them weren't all that skilled when it came to offensive or defensive moves. "How long have you been training?"

"Oh, gosh, years. I started as a kid then gave it up. Came back to it in my late teens and found I really hadn't forgotten the moves." She grinned. "I've been trying to talk some of my colleagues into getting in on it with me. We train the Kitty Cats in basic self-defense, not that our security team would ever let anything happen to them, but I just love how accessible Jujitsu is and I think a lot of the girls would do well."

"How'd you get started at Cowan Enterprises?" He'd never experienced a Kitty Cat party firsthand, but he'd seen enough press to know what they were all about.

"Oh, it was a total fluke that Sabine found me when she did. I wasn't even looking for a job at the time because I was still in school...drowning in student loans and convinced that if I just kept getting more letters behind my name, I'd find my dream job and make a killing." Cammie took a sip of her water. "We just happened to be at the same restaurant, sitting a table apart. I overheard her mention to the person she was with that she had specifically ordered the only thing on the menu that didn't have shellfish because she always had a weird kind of reaction to them. I knew the chef there and also knew that the odds were pretty good that she'd be eating something that had come in contact with shellfish, so I popped into the kitchen to make sure my friend knew he had a customer with a possible allergy."

"That was very considerate of you."

"I was looking out for my friend as much as Sabine, I guess. He didn't need bad press at his place of work." Cammie lifted one shoulder like what she had done was no big deal. "Sabine found out that I'd intervened, and a few days later she tracked me down and offered me a job as her PA."

"You gave up on school?"

"No, I finished." Cammie waved her hand like it was no big deal. "Sabine was really flexible, and I wrapped up my PhD a few months ago."

"I'm impressed!" Zane whistled. "We have a doctor in the house!"

"A doctor of literature. I can autopsy a classic in record time." Cammie laughed. "I've got an obscene amount of debt, but Sabine is very generous with my salary and bonuses, so I should be able to pay it off at some point in my life."

And yet she'd given up a five-thousand-dollar chip. Anther baffling rush of pride warbled through Zane's body. Cammie had stood by her principles in rejecting Haversmith's attempt to buy her. She'd discarded the chip like it was no big deal. That spoke of a truly solid set of morals.

Zane didn't really know this woman. He had no right to be invested in her future — not like a significant other should be — yet he had all these warm and fuzzy gurgles happening in his gut that had nothing to do with being hungry. Zane gulped down his water, draining the glass so he could banish the flutters in his stomach and clear his head. Cammie didn't want commitment and neither did he. Commitment came with complications. It came with the expectation for delving deep into each other's lives. He wasn't prepared to let anyone, especially not someone like Cammie, into his dark world.

"Crazy, isn't it?" He cleared a lingering lump from his throat. "I know a few people who went to school thinking they'd come out with a great job that would set them up for life, but all they have now is debt and minimum wage." He knew *of* a few people, mainly from investigations he'd done over the last year, but he didn't want to let on to Cammie how isolated he kept himself from others.

"What about you?" She poured him more water from the pitcher then topped up her own glass. "Did you go to school?"

"Did the military thing. Completed a few tours." Developed a reputation for sussing out intel, was recruited to be a spy, got captured and beaten to the brink of death, ended up in a coma for months then was honorably discharged. "Found out I was good at investigative work and had some connections, so I became a PI. So far so good." He still got wicked bad headaches occasionally that he knew were a result of the beating he'd taken. He drank a lot of the trauma away, which wasn't the best coping mechanism but seemed to work well enough. Every once in a while, he would lapse into a full-blown panic attack that would have him curled up in a corner, convinced that he was about to take another blow to the head. *Good times.*

"Have you worked on anything exciting? Anything super scandalous?" Cammie leaned forward, which did wonderful things to her cleavage and took Zane's mind completely off his past.

"More exciting than this?" He waved his hand around. "Nope." In truth, he'd been working pretty steadily on tracking people down who owed money for one reason or another. He'd done some repo jobs as well. So, when a cruise ship job had come up, he'd jumped at it, anything to shake up the monotony. He wasn't quite sure how Cal Underwood had found him. It certainly wasn't due to his outstanding reputation or track record, but the man had insisted Zane take the job and had offered premium pay and an all-expenses-paid trip. Who was Zane to turn down a rich guy with money to burn? "I'd imagine you have some pretty scandalous stories."

She tilted her head to the side and gave him a flirty side-eye. "I do, but my lips are sealed."

"Oh, I don't know... I've seen those lips of yours spread pretty wide." The heat between them ratcheted up a hundred-fold. "I might have some ways to get you to spill."

"I bet you do." She pressed her tits into the table so that her cleavage looked ready to explode and her nipples peeked at him from the table edge. "With the right kind of motivation, I might just—"

"There you two are!" Sherri breezed into the bistro in a flurry of heels, hair and manicured nails.

Cammie sat up spine straight, her cheeks flushed and eyes glassy. Zane coughed as he adjusted his achingly hard dick.

"I'm sorry to have to tell you that the workshop you both enrolled in has been postponed." Sherri exaggerated a frown. "But good news! There's a very special session that's being run by an industry superstar. I'm sure you've heard of Dr. Norma Rose, relationship specialist and dirty-talk guru?"

Zane looked at Cammie, who had an expression of total bewilderment on her face.

"Well, she has a spot for two and I thought, as one of our few committed couples on board, you would be perfect to join!" She tugged on Cammie's arm, somehow getting her to stand. "But you have to come now, because it's about to start."

Zane began to protest but Sherri cut him off. "Don't worry. I'll have your food delivered to you in the session. It's a special set-up...separate cubbies for total privacy. You'll be able to enjoy the session while eating your lunch...among other things." She winked but didn't slow down as she forcefully directed Cammie out of the restaurant, leaving Zane to follow after them, wondering if Cammie's head was going to explode with the sudden change of plans.

Chapter Seven

Dr. Norma Rose turned out to be a disembodied voice coming out of a small speaker mounted on the wall of the equally small cubby that Cammie and Zane had been ushered into. "Get comfortable, my lovelies," Dr Rose said in a sultry voice. "We will begin the Dirty Talk for Couples session in two minutes. Please know that your privacy is protected at all times while you are in your booth."

Cammie still didn't quite understand how it all happened, so kudos to Sherri for being a whirlwind of chaos management. If Cammie hadn't been so horrified, she might consider passing Sherri's name along to her boss, Sabine, because clearly the woman had talent as an event pusher. As it was, Cammie found herself in a couple's session that would require a level of intimacy that, once again, she felt was reserved for longer-term relationships, with a man she'd only just begun getting to know. Not that she didn't love a little dirty talk, but to be guided through it like this? With lights on and kinda sorta in public? No matter what privacy precautions were being taken — which Cammie didn't think were that cautious, based on how flimsy the walls seemed. *Um…no.* Dirty talk was for the heat of the moment. It was for couples who'd known each other longer than twenty-four hours. It was —

"Food's here!" Sherri yanked open the door and motioned the servers to bring in trays and trays of food.

Cammie looked over the small space. There was an oversized beanbag couch that seemed impossible for two full grown adults to squish into, but otherwise, the room was empty.

"It'll be like a picnic! Set the trays on the floor there," Sherri said to the servers. Then, turning to Cammie and Zane, she followed up with," Don't be shy, you two. Take a seat."

Cammie side-eyed the couch but Zane was already lowering himself into position, apparently fully game for whatever was about to happen.

"What's wrong, Cammie? Is this session not to your liking? I can always try to find you another —"

"No, no." The last thing Cammie wanted was for Sherri to find another session or whatever. At least this wasn't role playing. She could manage dirty talk with Zane. "This is fine. Really." She scooted over to the *couch*, weaving through the trays piled high with delicious-smelling food, then ungracefully lowered herself next to Zane.

She not only sunk into the beanbag but also toppled sideways like she had no control over her limbs. Zane chuckled softly and wrapped his arm around her to keep her upright.

It was very intimate but, strangely, also kinda nice. Being cuddled up with Zane wasn't the worse thing in the world. Maybe it wouldn't be such a bad session after all. Maybe they could ignore Dr. Sex-Talk Guru and just finish their meal together and continue talking. Maybe they could fake their way —

"Hello, Cammie and Zane!"

Cammie jolted and, somehow, managed to stifle a scream.

"I'm Dr. Rose, and I'll be your coach during parts of this session. Relax and get comfy." Her husky voice did nothing to sooth Cammie's nerves. "I'll give you direction in a few moments and walk you through the first exercise, then give feedback when you're done."

Cammie looked at Zane, whose eyes were crinkled and whose lips were curled into a grin like this was the funniest thing to ever happen to him. "Thanks, Dr. Rose," he said with a wink for Cammie. "We look forward to your feedback."

Worst idea ever! Not that it had been her idea but still... If only she'd asserted herself instead of letting Sherri bully her into this cubby. Seriously, what had come over her to let someone hijack her plans? Not that she'd had a to-do list for the day...not officially, anyway, but she had decided that she and Zane needed to get to know one another, since they were going to be spending so much time together investigating a murder! She'd chosen the bistro because the reviews had said that it had just the right amount of white noise to make first dates less awkward. But that damn event witch had sidelined Cammie's perfectly fine lunch idea for this...this shitshow of an experience.

Cammie shoved herself forward then grabbed one of the boxes of food. Maybe if her mouth was full of meat, she wouldn't have to participate and she could just pretend she was too busy eating to do anything the doctor said.

"Smart thinking." Zane grabbed another box. "We can incorporate food into our dirty talk."

"You're loving this, aren't you?" Cammie had the seasoned potato wedges, which were delightfully packed with flavor and just the right contrast of crunchy outside, soft inside, box in her hand. She shoved two wedges into her mouth, unconcerned by how that might look. If Zane couldn't handle her 'hangry' times, he wouldn't be able to handle her at all.

"Well, I figure we can make the best of it. Unless you want to go?" He motioned his thumb toward the door.

Cammie gave him a dark look but took the time to chew then swallow before responding. "And run the risk of the wrath of Sherri? I think not." She plucked a rib from his box. *Who knows what that woman could force us into next?* "And for the record, I don't have a problem with dirty talk."

"No?" Zane didn't seem surprised, just amused. "I'd imagine it's more the broad daylight, cubby in the middle of the ship, walls as thin as paper, people milling about outside, Dr. Dirty Talk listening in on us *and* giving pointers, that's got you all bothered."

He'd taken the words right out of her mouth, and she had to admit that it surprised her he'd been able to read her so well. She found herself wondering if she was so transparent or if he was just that good at investigating. Silence stretched between them, and she didn't know what to say, so she filled the gap by eating the juicy, tender, sauce-coated meat off one rib after another, matching Zane stride for stride in food consumption. It was all so damn delicious that she was almost distracted enough to enjoy the meal. The ribs were by far the best, though. They balanced tangy sweet and salty, then followed with a punch of heat that made Cammie moan.

"That's what I like to hear!" Dr. Rose's voice boomed over the speaker. "You two just couldn't wait for me, eh?"

Cammie nearly choked on her food. Zane passed her some sparkling water to help her get it all down her throat.

"We're enjoying our lunch, Dr. Rose. I hope that's okay." He wagged his eyebrows as he took a bite from one of the ribs, then made an exaggerated orgasm face that had Cammie snorting in the most embarrassing way.

"Oh yes, that's wonderful. Food can be such a sexy addition to our intimate moments."

Cammie wasn't sure that the way she was mowing down smoked meat and potatoes was exactly the epitome of sexy, but she was enjoying herself, at least for the moment, anyway.

"Let's get started," Dr. Rose said. "We'll begin with something easy." There was a rustle of paper. "Zane, we'll start with you."

"Sounds good, Doc!" Zane said between bites of a chicken leg.

"Excellent! I want you to take a minute to think of something you could say both about the food you're eating and about Cammie."

Cammie's eyes widened as she watched Zane's thought process roll over his face. He looked at his chicken leg, then at his saucy fingers, then at her. She was about to make a joke when his eyes hooded, and their gazes locked. A fizzle of heat pooled in Cammie's belly, and she put her next bite down.

"Are you ready, Zane?" Dr. Rose purred.

Zane tossed his chicken leg into an empty container, then wiped his hands on a napkin. "Ready."

"Lean toward Cammie. Get really close."

Zane shifted in the beanbag and nestled even closer to Cammie. His breath caressed her neck and it smelled like garlic and sauce and all the things that made her hungry for him. He cupped his hands under her chin and pushed her face up with his thumbs. It was a possessive gesture that made Cammie snap to attention. His eyes blazed with lust and his lips were almost touching hers. Her nipples budded and throbbed. Her pussy clenched and her body vibrated.

"Now, when you say your words, drop your voice so it sounds like a growl."

He tilted her head and nuzzled her earlobe. She shivered, her nipples tightened harder, her pussy quivered faster.

"I want to lick your sauce and nibble your skin. I want to feast on you, devour you whole, make you scream."

She believed him. Oh God…she wanted him to eat her whole. She wanted him to make her scream.

"Very good, Zane!" Dr. Rose's voice broke the spell that Zane was weaving. "Your growl is sensational!"

Zane pulled back so he could look Cammie in the eyes and what she saw, his expression of feral want, made her shiver all over again. He kissed her briefly. She tasted the barbecue sauce on his lips and wondered what it would feel like if he spread some sauce on her tits then sucked it off.

Zane let her face go. She couldn't move, stuck in a lusty fog of dirty thoughts and swirling pulses.

"Now, Cammie, your turn," Dr. Rose said.

At the sound of her name, Cammie snapped out of her head then prayed she didn't make a fool of herself. "Ready."

"Excellent! Now Cammie, I want you to demand something from Zane. Use your words and tell him exactly what you want him to do."

Okay, not hugely out of her comfort zone. She quickly glanced at the door. No lock. That made her uneasy. Anyone could walk in at any moment. She cringed. Zane started to wave like he was giving her permission to skip it.

But Cammie wasn't a quitter.

She could push herself out of her comfort zone a little if only because she really, really, wanted Zane to put his words to action.

Instead of just using words herself, she shifted the shoulder straps over her arms and yanked the halter portion of her dress down so her breasts were free. Zane's eyes nearly bulged out of his head.

"Zane," she purred as she dipped her fingers into the sauce from the ribs.

"That's it, Cammie, perfect tone! Keep going!" Dr. Rose said.

"I want you to kiss me…here." She rubbed the sauce over her nipples.

"Be explicit, Cammie. Now's not the time to be shy!" Dr. Rose sounded like a cheer captain.

Zane was already diving for her tits, one hand cupping so he could leverage her nipple to his lips while he slipped his other hand around her back and hoisted her closer to him.

"Zane," she groaned as his lips closed over her nipple. "Suck my tits…hard!"

"That's perfect, Cammie! Well done! I love your candor." Dr. Rose rustled a few papers again. "I'm going to pop over to another couple for a few minutes, but I'll leave you to practice using explicit language with one another, okay? Be back in a jiff!"

Zane was slurping and sucking, transitioning between one nipple to the next and Cammie couldn't help but writhe under his attention.

"Your tits are delicious," Zane growled.

"Zane," Cammie gasped, "I want you to lick my clit." While she did enjoy being a sub and taking orders, there was something about demanding Zane's attention that revved her up.

Zane shifted both hands under her ass and heaved her up onto the couch so he could crouch on the floor and have better access to her pussy. He licked her slit then latched onto her clit so hard that she jolted, somehow stifling a moan, swallowing it back so no one on the other side of the door would hear.

"Lick you like this?" He roughly poked and prodded at her aching nub before sucking her back into the warmth of his mouth once again.

"Yes! Yes! Just like that!" She tried to whisper but her voice was too rough sounding to be that quiet and she didn't care... *Oh God*...she didn't care at all, because Zane's tongue and lips and mouth were magic.

She teased her nipples, pulling and pinching, rubbing and flicking. They were sticky with sauce, so she gobbed some saliva on her fingers then coated herself, which just ended up making the sauce spread more.

Zane had a tight hold her on her ass with one hand. With the other hand, he parted her ass cheeks then sipped one sauced-up finger to her puckered hole. He spread the sauce all over then licked it off, delving his tongue as deep as he could go between her cheeks.

She arched into his mouth, her body almost convulsing as the layered sensations zapped her nerve endings to oblivion. When Zane tapped her clit with his finger, her orgasm detonated and her body, along with all coherent thought, absolutely exploded. Cammie bit down on her bottom lip to keep herself from screaming.

A loud knock rattled the door.

Cammie gasped but nothing could stop her from coming.

"What?" Zane growled, one hand out to keep the door handle from turning.

"Just checking to see if you want those trays of food removed!" Sherri boomed, clearly oblivious to what they were doing.

"No!" Cammie cried out.

"We're still eating!" Zane said.

As Cammie's orgasm rocked her entire body, so did the urge to burst out laughing. Her moans were punctuated with hiccupped giggles that made her sound like she was having some kind of fit.

Zane didn't relent until every last leg quivering spasm died, and finally, as the last of Cammie's laughing subsided, Dr. Rose came back on the speaker.

"Have you two been practicing?"

Cammie covered her mouth to keep herself from snorting through another bout of laughter.

"Yes, ma'am!" Zane wiped his mouth with a napkin and grinned as he helped Cammie sit up again.

"You two ready to take it to the next level?"

Zane cocked an eyebrow as if to say, you mean there's more? Which made Cammie cough through more giggles.

"Ready and willing!" Zane said.

"Wonderful! You two are such good sports." More paper rustling. "Okay, now, what I want you to do..."

Chapter Eight

Zane had definitely needed a shower after the dirty talk session, not just because his dick had been sticky from leftover barbecue sauce but because the words he'd spewed from his mouth all over Cammie had been down right filthy. He'd never uttered such nasty things in the presence of a woman before, or, for that matter, uttered them at all.

Considering how reluctant she'd been to do the session in the first place, Cammie had really gotten into it. She'd been so into it that they'd been seconds away from public sex, like, Cammie had been in the process of straddling him with a devious gleam in her eyes, when Dr. Rose had announced that they'd passed with flying colors, because, apparently, she'd been grading them. Then they'd been told to get out the hell out of the cubby so it could be cleaned before the next session started, which had sobered up their lust-clouded brains pretty quickly.

Cammie had decided to go to her room so she could shower and get ready for dinner. Formal dinner this time, because Zane had a lead on another one of their targets. Which, of course, reminded him that he'd done very little work of his own in the last twenty-four hours.

Before squeezing himself into his dinner suit, he decided to take a few minutes to try to make some progress in his case. He added notes about Bill Haversmith's appearance, estimated height, weight that kind of thing. The guy was slimy as fuck, but other than the reoccurring trips on Dark Matter cruises, there wasn't anything else pointing to Bill's involvement with the missing money. Since the man clearly had more money than he had use for — tossing Cammie five thousand dollars like it was nothing — it didn't make a whole lot of sense that he would be caught up in some kind of stealing scheme on board a ship, anyway. Unless the missing money was just sloppy counting or someone skimming off the top, that came from some other kind of business...like laundering.

If laundering was the game in play, Zane would look squarely at Captain Evans, since he'd boasted about knowing everything that happened on board his ship, working with Bill Haversmith in some way. It was possible that Captain Evans was moving money for Haversmith, having it cleaned through the casino, maybe. Zane had theories but no evidence or proof, so he really needed to get digging, because there were only a few days left of the cruise.

Much to Zane's surprise, while playing with Cammie in the dirty-talk session, Zane had realized another way to track money through the cruise line. He quickly built another algorithm. The casino seemed like the fastest way to clean money, but there was another way that would yield opportunities to skim off the top, and it could help them narrow down finding their missing man.

Checking the time, he finished typing the code then quickly put his suit on. He'd never owned anything super formal, so he'd only brought one pair of black slacks, a button-up turquoise shirt and a dinner jacket. He didn't think he'd need a tux but also wasn't sure if his attire was formal enough. Nothing he could do about it, though. Cammie would likely be dressed to kill, so she'd more than make up for his lack of style.

He checked his computer one more time, making sure things were running as they were supposed to before leaving. He was on his way to meet Cammie at her cabin, but as the elevator doors binged open, she was right there in front of him, and she looked stunning.

"Hi," she said, her dimples popping and eyes sparkling. "I thought I'd meet you halfway."

"You look amazing," Zane said. And she did. *Oh, fuck,* she did.

She was wearing a slinky black dress that hugged every one of her curves just like he wanted to. There was a long slit up each side so that he could see her upper thighs and a very low dipping front that showcased her beautiful cleavage.

"Thanks," she said with a giggle before doing a little twirl. "I wasn't sure how formal a formal dinner is on a cruise, so I thought I'd play it safe with my little black dress."

Zane stepped into the elevator with her, his hand on her lower back. "There's nothing safe about that dress."

He leaned down to kiss just below her earlobe then did it again when she shivered.

They stepped off the elevator together and didn't get more than a few feet toward the restaurant when the booming voice of Bill Haversmith assaulted them.

"Look who it is!" Bill beelined right for them, his face a glossy shade of red. "My good friends Cammie and…er…what did you say your name was, fella?" Bill had already wrapped his arm around Cammie's shoulder.

"Zane Roberts."

"So it is, Zane…right, right." Bill began to walk, with Cammie trapped under his arm, toward some sort of greeting line. "I want to introduce you to the captain. Captain Evans—"

In an expert maneuver, Cammie dipped then shifted, extracting herself from Bill's grasp just in time to come face-to-face with Captain Evans.

"Hello, Captain," Cammie said, her voice as cool and smooth as ice. "Nice to see you again."

"And you, Miss Sheppard. I trust you're feeling well." If Captain Evans was surprised to see Zane and Cammie with Bill Haversmith, he didn't show it. "Zane." He nodded toward Zane as if to say, 'glad to see you're sticking with Cammie'.

"Evans, I didn't realize you'd already met this beauty." Bill, just seeming to realize that Cammie was no longer under his arm, looked slightly bewildered to find her holding hands with Zane instead. The man was definitely not sober.

"Oh, yes, we've met." Captain Evans didn't elaborate, and Zane could tell that Cammie was on the verge of sniping something but somehow managed to hold herself back. He didn't blame her for being pissed at the captain, considering he'd all but called her a lunatic. "Bill, will you be joining us at my table tonight?"

"Yes, indeed, sir!" Bill waved one of the servers over. "Please make sure there's room at the captain's table for my friends, Cammie and Zane."

Captain Evans frowned. He opened his mouth like he was ready to argue Bill's impromptu invite to his private table.

"No worries, Cap!" Bill draped his arm over Captain Evan's shoulder then leaned in close. "We can always talk business another time." It was clear he was attempting to keep his voice low, but his volume button was out of control.

"Captain Evans..." A server swept up with a beaming smile. "Your table is ready."

And just like that, they were all ushered toward a private room at the back of the dining room, and Zane wasn't sure if it was the best thing that could have happened for his investigation or the worst.

"Is this really happening?" Cammie whispered to him.

He didn't get a chance to answer because it really was happening, and they were directed to seats near the head of the table, close to Bill and the captain. The table seated eight, and as more people filed into the room, clearly the upper echelon of the cruise, Cammie looked at him with wide eyes and clear confusion.

He knew what was going through her head. How were they going to find their next target if they were stuck at this table? The captain would get suspicious if Zane and Cammie stuck to their original plan, which had consisted of eyeballing all the men in attendance until they found their target, then joining his table so they could confirm who he was. Maybe it wasn't the most sophisticated plan, but it would have worked, while still giving them time to be together, which Zane was quickly coming to accept, was what he really wanted to be doing with Cammie. "I'll figure it out."

The wild look in Cammie's eyes softened and she nodded.

"Hi, I'm Jasper Haversmith." A younger guy who, if Zane were to guess, was in his early twenties, slid into the chair next to Zane then offered his hand.

"Zane and Cammie," Zane said as he shook Jasper's hand.

Cammie gave a little wave. "You're Bill's son?"

"That's right." He adjusted his chair. "I see you've gotten yourselves caught up in my father's sticky web. Welcome to the party." He said this with a wide smile and a wink, but Zane heard an edge to his words. Jasper definitely had a chip on his shoulder where his dad was concerned. Just how big of a chip, Zane was curious to find out.

"Do you and your dad often travel on kink cruises together?" Cammie went where Zane wasn't prepared to go right away, but she did it with a wink of her own and a smile that showcased her dimples, a feature that would disarm any man.

"Hardly." Jasper rolled his eyes. "Dad considers this trip his way of making a man out of me." He air-quoted the last few words. "He says it's important for networking, but I think he really means he wants me to—"

"Jasper, are you telling tales again?" Bill was all bluster and boom, his voice drowning out every other conversation happening as new guests arrived and took their seats. "That boy is full of stories. He wanted to be a journalist, if you can imagine." Bill leaned close to Cammie like she was some kind of confidante. "But I straightened him out right quick. None of that liberal nonsense happening with the Haversmith name, I tell ya!"

Cammie shifted in her seat, moving as far away from Bill as she could get without ending up on Zane's lap. "Oh? I don't think journalism is that bad of a career choice."

"Now, now, little lady, we both know that your boss takes issue with those rascals. Doesn't she make a promise to all her clients that discretion is priority number one?" He tapped his head. "I've done my research since we last talked. Sabine Cowan is a ball breaker when it comes to the press."

"Well, yes, Sabine does value her client's privacy, and it is our number one priority." Cammie shrugged. "We don't allow reporters into our parties or anywhere else if we can help it. But that doesn't mean I have anything against journalists."

"I like you already, Cammie." Jasper raised his glass of wine to her.

She raised her glass of water back.

"Psh." Bill waved her off. "You've met my good friend, Elm?"

A tall, broad-chested man wearing a cowboy hat entered the private room just as Bill introduced him.

"Did someone say my name?" He was just as loud as Bill, bellowing so the entire room stopped talking to look up at him. "Captain Evans, good to see you again." Elm shook hands with the captain before heading to his seat on the other side of the table. "Jasper," he said with a slight nod.

"You remember this little beauty, don't ya, Elm?" Bill said as he put a meaty hand on Cammie's shoulder.

"Hands off, Mr. Haversmith." Cammie was all sugar and spice. "My boyfriend, Zane, isn't too keen on sharing."

"Oh, ho! I do love a woman who speaks her mind." Bill lifted his hand, making a big show of it to the table, who all laughed like he'd just told the joke of the year.

"Miss Sheppard," Elm said with a tip of his hat. "Wonderful to see you again." He leaned forward hand extended to Zane. "You must be the boyfriend."

"I must be," Zane said with a smile. Even pretending he was man enough to be Cammie's boyfriend had him flying high. He shook Elm's hand over the table. "Zane Roberts."

"Good to meet you." Elm slipped his hat off then hung it on the back of his chair before taking his seat. "Bill, you been imbibing all afternoon?"

"That I have, old friend." Bill raised his glass of whiskey. "You better catch up quick."

Elm barked a laugh but picked up his own whiskey and tapped his glass to Bill's. "Bottom's up!"

Conversations picked up again, a white noise that was hard to pull apart. Cammie was chit chatting with the woman to Elm's left, across from her, while Bill, Elm and the captain were seemingly reminiscing about a past cruise.

"What do you do, Zane?" Jasper said as the first course arrived.

"Investment banker," Zane lied.

"Ah, I see. That's why Dad's latched himself to you." Jasper downed his wine then motioned for a refill.

"I think that has more to do with Cammie than me." Zane laughed. "Not sure your father is too keen on investment bankers in general."

"Well, not if you're trying to get him investing in Dark Matter's cruise line. That's for sure." Jasper snorted.

Zane decided in that very moment to show his cards. "Why's that? Because of the money leak?"

Jasper nearly choked on his wine. "You are good!" He leaned closer. "I didn't think anyone knew about how badly the cruise line was hemorrhaging money. It's all Dad talks about lately. In fact, knowing my dad, this trip is probably his way of convincing the board that Dark Matter's cruise line is ripe for a takeover."

"He brought his board on this trip?"

"Yes, sir, he did. Bunch of old womanizers as it is." He tipped his glass toward Elm. "That's one of them right there."

"Is this Elm's first trip on one of these cruises?"

"As far as I know, he's only been on one other. The first time Dad experienced a fetish cruise, Elm was with him. Since then, Dad has been a regular traveler on board Dark Matter cruises. He says it's because it's one of a kind, and he likes the amenities." Jasper rolled his eyes. "I know my dad, though, and he's not one to bet on a sinking ship—but he is one to dismantle it."

"I'd just heard that they money seemed to be siphoning out somewhere. I didn't know the company was doing that poorly. I mean, a takeover... Wow!"

"Where there's smoke, there's fire." Jasper shoved his salad to the side and replaced it with his wine glass, clearly giving up the pretense of eating. "Why do you think the good ol' captain is kissing my dad's ass? He's got a vested interest in keeping this cruise line going."

"What kind of vested interest?"

"Cammie, baby, I heard the craziest story earlier." Bill's booming voice pulled Zane's attention away from Jasper, not so much because of how loud the man was but because there was an edge that hadn't been there before.

"I can only imagine," Cammie drawled.

"Yeah, I heard that one of the sexy little waitresses in the casino found a five-thousand-dollar chip on her tray." He leaned in close to Cammie with narrowed eyes. "Right around the time you were leaving with the five-thousand-dollar chip I gave ya."

"Did you see the heels those girls were wearing? A five-thousand-dollar tip isn't nearly enough, in my opinion." Cammie stared right back at him. "You filthy rich men should think about being so generous with your tips, especially since you're so generous with your hands."

The table had fallen silent, so Cammie's words hung over the room like a cloud. Zane felt a crackle of danger and the testosterone seemed to skyrocket. He shifted his chair back in case he needed to get Cammie out of her seat and out of the room fast. It was hard to tell when rich men with power would decide to use it, especially after a gauntlet had been thrown down.

"I love your sass, girl!" Bill barked a laugh and smacked the table so hard that the glasses shook all the way down the length. "That's right! All you filthy rich gentlemen sitting at this table! You better be givin' generous tips, or you'll have Cammie to answer to."

Zane relaxed back into his seat then reached under the table to squeeze Cammie's knee. She flashed him a wicked grin before taking a bite of her salad, and he realized once again just how lucky he was to have met

Cammie. She was a boss in her own right and used to dealing with men like Bill.

He was grinning when Zane turned back to finish his conversation with Jasper but the seat next to him was empty.

Chapter Nine

Dinner was an ordeal, as far as Cammie was concerned. She'd figured out right away that Zane probably needed to be at that table with some of the most powerful men on the ship because of his mysterious investigation. She'd caught enough of his conversation with Bill's son to get the drift that whatever Zane was hunting had to do with missing money, which made sense because the CEO of Dark Matter Inc., Cal Underwood, was only ever concerned with money—making it and not losing it. If there was theft going on aboard his cruise line, Cal would be all over figuring out why and how to stop it, and if he couldn't stop it, he'd cut the cruise line free and sell it to the highest bidder.

For the rest of the meal, she'd found herself scrutinizing the men around her, wondering if they were up to no good in ways she hadn't considered. Was the captain involved in some kind of money scheme? Obviously, she thought the man was an ass for not believing her about the dead guy in her room, but was it also possible that his refusal to believe her wasn't just him being patronizing? Had he been trying to cover up something else? Maybe he knew exactly what had happened in her room because the dead guy was all tangled in Zane's case and the captain was entwined with that scheme as well.

She also didn't believe for one hot second that Chief Ross was on the up and up. He'd insisted he'd checked the cameras on her deck, when Cammie knew for certain that there were no cameras on her deck. She was trained to suss out little details like that, thanks to her job, and she'd noted right away that there was no surveillance anywhere on the floor where her cabin was. There was a metal plate where a camera could, in theory, have been, but there was nothing there now.

As she and Zane had been saying their goodbyes after dinner, Chief Ross had come storming into the private room looking like his ass was on fire. When he'd caught sight of Cammie, he'd given a somewhat hilarious double take that had him clamping his lips shut and cutting off whatever it was he'd been about to say to the captain. After some awkward hellos, and goodbyes, Cammie and Zane had finally been able to leave, and she was bursting to talk it all out with Zane but he, apparently, had other plans.

"I have an idea," he said as he guided her toward the elevators.

Her mind immediately went to their unfinished sexual business from earlier. She was already pumped up and full of adrenaline. Sex play had been fun during the dirty talk session, but Cammie was definitely ready for a full fucking. Besides, she was totally amped from her whirling thoughts and the bizarre dinner with Bill and his pals.

"Since we've missed our chance to find Tony LaRoch at his table, let's pop up to his deck and knock on his door. There's a good chance he'll go back up to his cabin to change into something more comfortable now that dinner is over."

Cammie's dirty thoughts stutter-stopped... She'd been, once again, fully in gutter brain mode while Zane had been focused on solving her mystery. Her cheeks heated and she had to work really hard to keep herself from giggling like a maniac.

"You okay?" Zane glanced at her, one eyebrow crooked.

Cammie slipped her arm around his, her eyes wide, in, what she hoped, was a purely innocent look. "All good."

Zane eyed her for a second or two longer before continuing. "It's a bit risky to be snooping around on a deck that isn't ours, which is why I haven't suggested it before, but I think we can pull it off if the steward isn't around." They stepped onto the elevator together and were luckily alone.

"We need a cover story for Tony and for the steward, if we run into one on that deck...preferably the same story," Cammie said as she watched Zane punch the deck number.

"Good thinking. We got lost?" Zane gave her a lopsided grin. "Or we're old friends of Tony's?"

"That won't work if we actually find Tony." Cammie's thoughts circled back to the gutter, just as the doors binged open. She kept the grin off her face. "Follow my lead." She scanned the hallway. There was not a soul to be seen. *Perfect!* "What room is Tony's?"

"First one on the right." Zane pointed to the door immediately next to them.

Cammie yanked Zane out of the elevator. "Ravage me." She slipped her hands around Zane's shoulders and hoisted herself up his body so she could kiss him.

Zane didn't waste a moment. Whether he understood her strategy or not, he was all in. He gripped her waist, yanking her closer as he crushed his lips to hers. She dragged one hand down his shirt, popping buttons open on her way to his belt. He unzipped part of her dress so that the shoulder straps began to fall. All the while they kissed furiously, tongues entangled, probing, lips devouring. She maneuvered them in front of Tony's door then fell backward, dragging Zane along with her so there was a thump of her ass hitting the door, then her elbow, then her head, then —

"Can I help you?"

Zane clenched her waist and kept her from falling backward into the room. Cammie gasped as she tore herself away from Zane's kiss. Despite it all being a ploy, her brain was foggy and full of lust, so it took her a second to be able to focus on the man who'd opened the door. "What are you doing in our room?"

The man, presumably Tony, shook his head. "You're mistaken, Miss. This is my cabin."

He was older than the man she'd found on her floor but there was a slight resemblance. Not enough to mistake him for the dead guy, though.

"Oh my gosh!" She playfully smacked Zane on the chest. "We got off on the wrong deck! How embarrassing."

"Sorry to disturb you," Zane chuckled. "We got a little carried away." He offered his hand. "Zane Roberts."

"No worries! Tony LaRoch." He shook Zane's hand then turned to Cammie.

"Cammie Sheppard, and I am very sorry for this." She let him take her hand but pulled away when he started to lift it to his mouth. Old-fashioned *and* smarmy. *Wonderful.*

"Absolutely nothing to be sorry for. These things happen in the heat of the moment." Tony motioned behind him. "My wife and I are always looking for another couple to join our play."

"Thanks, but no." Zane, quick on his feet as usual, managed to respond before Cammie could even form a coherent thought. "We're only just discovering each other, and I'm not one for sharing." He tightened his arm around Cammie's waist. "Maybe the next cruise."

"Of course!" Tony chuckled. "Well, if you change your mind, you know where we are."

"We sure do!" Cammie's voice came out in a squeak.

Tony closed the door and Cammie had to cover her mouth to keep herself from laughing too loudly. "That was not what I was expecting," she whispered.

"Me neither." Without being asked, Zane zipped up her dress.

"Thanks." Her cheeks were hot, and her heart thundered both from the inferno of her lust and the interaction with Tony LaRoch.

Zane buttoned up his shirt then straightened his jacket as they waited for an elevator to arrive. "I have half a mind to take you back to my cabin for real and finish what we started."

She bit her lip as she turned to face him, ready to climb back onto him and do exactly that right there when the doors opened to an almost-full car.

"Going up?" A man put his hand on the doors to keep them open. "There's room. Hop on board!"

When Zane hit another deck that wasn't either of theirs, Cammie realized that he was planning on knocking on the last man's door...and the prospect of make-out ploy round two had her body coiling all over again. She snuck him a wicked grin and he returned it with a wink. Maybe being spontaneous was the way to go after all. Screw planning every last detail to death. Cammie was beginning to see the benefits of zigzagging through all her straight lines.

When the doors opened, Cammie practically skipped out, dragging Zane behind her. She was about to turn, ready to launch back into their hot and heavy play when someone cleared their throat.

"Hello there! What can I do for you two?" The steward was all smiles, just like Ben, but he was older and far more suspicious, despite his friendly greeting. "Did you get off on the wrong deck?" He knew right away that they didn't belong there.

"Oh no...ah, we're just checking up on a friend. He wasn't at dinner." Cammie's voice cracked a little which made the steward's eyes narrow even more.

"And what's your friend's name?"

"Salis Collie," Zane said, his voice as smooth as silk. Cammie looked up at him, admiring his calm demeanor. "His room is right there." Zane pointed a few doors down the hall.

"Oh yes, Mr. Collie." The steward frowned. "I'm afraid Mr. Collie isn't in right now."

"I hope he's okay." Cammie put on a mask of concern. Seriously, she deserved an Oscar for her performance, considering how badly her body was vibrating from all her pent-up lust. "I know he wasn't feeling well yesterday."

"Really?" The steward looked genuinely concerned. "He hasn't been in his cabin since departure, but I assumed he was just out and about. I should check the infirmary." He shimmied past Zane. "If you'll excuse me."

Cammie looked sharply at Zane and hoped he got her drift. Salis hadn't been back to his room because he was probably dead.

"We'll come with you," Zane said, leaving no room for argument as he entwined his fingers with Cammie's and kept pace with the steward.

* * * *

While the infirmary had a few men who were clearly suffering from something, there was no sign of Salis Collie, or at least, no sign of anyone who looked remotely like the dead guy Cammie had found on her floor.

Which meant that they had one missing man who fit the description, at least on paper, of the body she'd found.

"It's him." Cammie's whisper came out like a growl.

Zane lifted a hand to quiet her so he could presumably eavesdrop on the hushed conversation between the nurse and the steward. Cammie couldn't hear shit and she was impatient to get Zane alone so she could share her theories with him, about the captain, about the fact that Salis Collie was her guy.

"Good news." The steward returned, his hands already motioning for them to exit the infirmary. "Mr. Collie hasn't been here, which means he's likely enjoying all the amenities available on the cruise."

Cammie and Zane moved into the hallway. "Is that normal?" Zane asked. "Do people often spend all their time participating in events and never return to their cabins?" He squeezed Cammie's waist and hauled her closer to his side. "Gosh, honey, we're missing out!"

"Oh yes, very normal. Many guests like to use every available minute to enjoy the perks that come with a lot of the packages." The steward led them to the elevator. "I hope you're able to reconnect with your friend." He ushered them on but didn't follow. "And do enjoy the cruise!" He waved and smiled as the doors closed.

Cammie spun to face Zane. "Salis is our guy!"

"Whoa, there, slow down."

"What? Why? It all makes sense...and the captain has to know something. He's involved in all this, I'm sure of it." Cammie's words tumbled out until she was out of breath.

"The captain is definitely involved in something." Zane stepped off the elevator as the doors slid open. They'd landed on his deck. "I need to check something in my cabin. You coming?" He held his hand out to Cammie.

She wanted to keep going. She wanted to tell someone what they'd discovered, but she couldn't tell the captain. She couldn't she tell Chief Ross, because the head of security was as shady as they come. Ben, her steward? Could she tell him?

What would he do?

He'd want to tell the captain and the chief of security.

Cammie's bubble of urgency deflated, and she let out a sigh.

"Lead the way," she said as she accepted Zane's hand.

"I ran an algorithm while we were at dinner. I think it might help." He opened his cabin door then motioned her in first. "Or at least it might give us some answers before we do anything rash."

Rash? Suggesting that Cammie would do something reckless? She opened her mouth to argue, but he beat her to it.

"Not that I think you're being rash." He grimaced slightly as he typed a few things into his laptop. "But look." He turned the screen toward her.

She saw a list of names.

"It occurred to me when we were in our Dirty Talk cubby that they're taking attendance at the sessions, which makes sense. They're collecting data about what works and what doesn't work, what guests want and what they aren't so keen on. I built an algorithm to isolate the guests who signed up but never showed up for different events." He pointed to Salis Collie's name. "Salis has signed up for at least fifty different sessions."

Cammie followed Zane's finger along the data then deflated even more.

"And he's shown up for all them so far."

"Right." Cammie slumped onto Zane's bed. "He's not missing and he's not dead. He's just horny."

Chapter Ten

"But I do think you're on to something. There's a connection between the dead guy in your room and my case." Zane clicked a few more tabs, closing the list he'd just opened. "I can do a search through the crew database." He should have started with the staff, and he was kicking himself now for not even considering it. He'd believed that Cammie had seen a dead guy in her room almost from the beginning, but he'd focused on the travelers rather than the staff because…well…because he was a jerk. He assumed that their cases were separate and that there was no way that whatever happened in her room was connected to missing money on board the ship. It had been short-sighted of him, if only because he hadn't remembered seeing anyone who might resemble Cammie's description…when he'd skimmed and scanned the staff photos back at home, weeks ago. "Each staff has a profile and a photo."

He started scrolling, waiting as the photos loaded one by one. Cammie's eyes darted quickly from frame to frame. He scrolled lower, giving her time to look at every one that came up.

On the third page, his eyes immediately plucked a guy out and he cursed under his breath. Dark hair, blue eyes, young, totally could be Cammie's dead body.

Seconds later, Cammie's gasp confirmed it for Zane.

"That's him." She jabbed her finger at the screen.

"You're sure?" Zane shifted the tab so that she could read the man's identifying information.

"Yes, positive!" She leaned closer. "Francesco Maccino, twenty-two, five-foot-nine, one-hundred and seventy pounds."

"Not reported missing," Zane noted. "Which means that you were right all along. Our cases have got to be connected. Someone is covering up Francesco's death, and it's got to be someone working on the ship, because there's no way this guy hasn't been missed."

"Where does he work?" Cammie motioned for Zane to move his cursor so she could continue reading. "Sous chef, event staging, tech crew and look…" She pointed to the next line. "He's been on every cruise for the last six months. No breaks."

Which means he'd been on every cruise with Bill Haversmith. Wheels were turning, connections forming. Zane's brain jumped all over the place, trying to link more dots.

"We have to tell someone!" Cammie jumped up from the bed then immediately sat back down again. "I just don't know who we can trust."

"Exactly, so we don't tell anyone." When she started to argue, Zane touched her hand. "*Yet*. We don't tell anyone, *yet*. We've got to give this a little more time to play out. Someone is moving behind the scenes, thinking they're invisible, and now that we're watching, we're going to catch them in the act."

"The act of what?" Cammie shook her head. "What if they're going to murder someone else? Shouldn't we alert security? Maybe not Dilan but someone?"

He noted that she hadn't suggested the captain, and he could tell by her expression that she knew going to the security chief wasn't going to work, either. She'd made all the same connections as he had. She wanted a solution — he understood that — but with the way things were, not knowing who was involved, they'd have to wait.

"Let's consider the evidence we have so far." Zane pushed his laptop to the side then arranged himself, somewhat awkwardly, on the bed so he could face her. "We have a dead man but no body to prove it."

Cammie opened her mouth but closed it just as quickly. She let out a sigh that was edged with exhaustion, and he had to wonder if she was getting tired of him or the situation.

"We have a crew member who matches the description but doesn't appear to be reported missing, although we don't know for sure if anything is happening behind the scenes to look for him. It is possible that the crew is aware and that they're searching for Francesco without alerting the guests, so as not to induce panic."

Cammie nodded but kept her lips sealed and her eyes narrowed.

"We have missing money from six separate trips. One point one million, to be exact." He hadn't told Cammie any of the details of his investigation before this, so her eyes widened when he revealed just how much money had been stolen. "I figure the money is being siphoned in small increments from the casino." He pointed to the computer. "Or from the add-ons that guests purchase once they're on board." His algorithm had also created a list of guests who'd dropped considerable amounts of cash on amenities that were not included in the price of the ticket. If money was being laundered through one or both of these zones, it wouldn't be hard to skim off the top as well. "And we have a 'people of interest' list that starts with the captain and includes Bill Haversmith and the security chief."

"You think the captain is involved?" Cammie didn't look shocked so much as impressed, which only confirmed what Zane had already guessed. Cammie understood way more than he'd given her credit for, and she'd definitely connected more dots quicker than he had.

"I think there's a reason why he brushed you off, and it's not because he's an idiot." Zane nodded. "By Bill Haversmith's own admission, he and the captain have business to discuss. I suspect that business involves my case in some way."

"And Chief Ross?" Cammie asked. "You think he's involved too somehow?"

"It would make sense. Maybe he's strongarming the captain or maybe he's just one of the captain's henchmen. If our hypothesis is true and the dead man in your room and the missing money are connected, then it's possible that Dilan Ross is connected in some way with Francesco's death."

"Murder," Cammie corrected.

"Not sure we can say that conclusively." Zane lifted his hand for her to hear him out. "Did you see any signs that might indicate murder? A stab or gunshot wound? Ligature marks?"

"I'm not exactly a coroner." Cammie shook her head. "But it didn't look like his death had been violent. Could have been a drug overdose or poison. He kinda looked surprised? Or my imagination is totally out of control and I'm remembering wrong." She sighed.

"Or it's possible that Francesco died by accident or even natural causes, somehow ended up in your room, then disappeared. It's possible someone is covering up his death, if only to keep the other guests comfortable and unaware."

Cammie seemed to roll that information around in her head for a bit. "That's not what my gut is saying."

"Mine either, but we need proof, and we need to get close to our suspects and dig deeper."

"Why put the dead body in my room in the first place? The odds of me stumbling onto it would be pretty high." Cammie tapped her finger to her lips. "There's no security camera on my floor."

Zane blinked hard. Of course she'd sussed that out already. "None at all?" He'd figured the cameras had been disabled.

"No sign of any, but there is a metal plate where one could have been." Cammie pointed to Zane's computer. "You should add Sherri to your list. She would know if one of her team was missing. Even if she's not directly connected to whatever he's working on, one of her managers would have reported him as a no-show for work. That's the way it goes, in my experience, anyway. There's always a chain of command, and information flows both up and down that chain. Everyone is accounted for and needs to check in regularly to make sure the event goes smoothly. On a ship like this, things have to be very tight. Everyone has their job to do. Someone knows Francesco is missing."

Zane added Sherri to his mental list of suspects and planned to take a few moments to review her staff profile more closely like he'd already done for the captain and Chief Ross. "We've been into the infirmary and saw no one matching the description of your dead man there, so Francesco isn't recovering from something. We can rule out him just being sick."

'Because he's dead,' Cammie's eyes said to him.

"It's part of the process. We have to eliminate all the possible places Francesco could be if he were alive and just sick, even if we know he's actually dead," he explained.

"This is a huge ship! He could be anywhere." Cammie let out an exasperated huff. "How in the world are we going to look in every possible place that Francesco, if he were alive, could be?"

"We check the staff cabins for him. If he's not there, then we know that someone should be able to tell us where he is." He lifted his hand. "But we can't be too obvious about asking about him, because if he has been murdered, we don't want to alert the wrong people that we're sniffing around."

"What do we do now?" Cammie lifted both hands in a helpless gesture. "I know you say wait, but I need to do something. I need a plan."

"*We* need a plan." Zane pulled his computer back on his lap. "So, let's come up with one together."

"That just so happens to be something I'm good at." Cammie beamed, her eyes alight like things were finally making sense to her.

"I know." Zane winked and Cammie's dimples popped, which did a lot of funny things to Zane's body—first and foremost making his heart putter a little more hectically at the idea of doing something to make Cammie happy.

And that's when he knew, with gut-sinking awareness, that he'd crossed the line at some point and let Cammie past his armor.

Not good for my heart. Nope. Not good at all.

"We need to confirm that Salis Collie is where he's supposed to be." Zane cleared his throat and tried commanding his heart to settle the fuck down. Not that his heart was in any state to listen to reason, but seriously, it had only been meant to be a fling. He'd only known Cammie for a little more than twenty-four hours and his heart was all haywire over her? Seriously? He hadn't come on the cruise to find love or even to find a connection. Meeting up with Cammie right out of the gate had been a bonus, but it wasn't supposed to be more than that. That's all Cammie had said she'd wanted—a fling, short term—over in five days. Christ, that's all Zane had wanted, as well. So, what had changed?

Too many things. His former therapist would be delighted, especially since Zane was completely baffled by how quickly Cammie had infiltrated his defenses— ones that had worked for years to keep people at a distance.

Zane had never been one to believe in love at first sight. Lust at first sight, absolutely, but never the whole heart taking a nosedive into the heart of another person. Nope. That kind of shit was not for him.

And yet, here he was, totally enthralled by Cammie.

"Anyone could, in theory, say he was at a session just as a cover, so let's confirm he's actually where he's supposed to be." Zane tapped a few things into his computer, trying to keep himself hyper-focused on the task at hand and not on how close Cammie was to him or how badly he wanted to wrap her up in his arms and roll her under his body.

"Let's figure out what he signed up for tonight." Cammie scrunched in closer to Zane, and he had to stifle the urge to move his arm so he could cuddle her onto his lap.

He refocused on his screen and tried not to take too many deep breaths to soak in her intoxicating scent.

Salis Collie was supposed to be at the Whips and Chains Dance Party in an hour. Without much thinking involved, and just a few clicks, Zane registered himself, along with Cammie, minutes before the registration window closed.

They had to figure out what to wear, because, of course, there was a dress code—one that required very little clothing from what Zane could tell. He didn't mind some risk-taking, but this time he might have pushed his own boundaries a little too far. He definitely should have checked out the photos before he'd pushed the button.

"I might need to go shopping," Cammie said as she gazed at the photos of past parties. "I brought a few things that could work, but I'm in the mood for something different. There's a fetish wear store on the promenade deck."

Cammie, on the other hand, seemed totally in her element.

"You're not freaked out by having to dress up?" Zane closed his laptop, resigned to the reality that he was going to have to go shopping with Cammie if he wanted to attend the party with her. Unlike her, he hadn't brought anything that could work.

"Nope." Her eyes crinkled with her grin. "This is totally my thing. Kitty Cat parties are all about dressing up."

He held his hand out for her to take as he heaved himself off the bed. "Then I guess you're going to have to find something that'll work on a bear like me."

She laid her hand in his, her eyes gleaming. "That is definitely something I can do."

Chapter Eleven

Fetish-wear shopping alone had always given Cammie a thrill, but fetish-wear shopping with a lover? Unstoppable shivers all over. The little boutique store had a surprising selection of outfits and costumes that had all titillated her, but she'd gone with a more traditional look, if there was such a thing, for both her and Zane...leather and metal. Not real leather, of course, which would have cost a fortune, but the clothing was very well made and the outfits both she and Zane had settled on fit like they were destined for them.

Zane tugged at the black paneled kilt that came mid-thigh on him and showcased his muscular legs. "You're sure this doesn't look ridiculous?"

Cammie appraised him with every ounce of lust she felt blasting out of her eyes. "Oh, hell no!" From the moment he'd put on the kilt, her pussy had been on fire and aching for his cock. "You look like a beast, a warrior."

He'd pushed back on the fishnet shirt as well as the alternative leather strap getup that would have framed his chest exquisitely and instead had opted for a gray linen shirt that seemed to be missing almost all its buttons. It did little to cover his upper body, but did, indeed, give him a rough-and-tumble Highlander look. Zane had it tucked into the kilt like he was in some kind of weird prep-school. She closed the gap between them then tugged one side of the shirt out while at the same time slipping her other hand over his pec to tease his nipple.

Zane growled and attempted to scoop her up, but she slipped away quickly, dancing just out of reach. "Don't you want to see *my* outfit?"

She'd put on his bathrobe before exiting his restroom, partly because she wanted to keep her outfit a surprise until the last possible minute and partly because the idea of wearing it in public was giving her heart a bit of a flutter. Sure, she'd worn fetish wear before but nothing even close to this. As soon as she'd seen the dress, she'd known immediately that Zane would love it, and she'd plucked it off the rack before he could see what she'd found.

"Hell yes! Show me." His eyes shone with a hunger that made Cammie's whole body quiver.

Her fingers trembled as she undid the tie around her waist then sucked in a deep breath before letting the robe slide off her shoulders to pool at her feet.

Zane took her all in. His eyes went from the tight collar encircling her throat to the way the leather corset squeezed and lifted her tits so that her nipples were almost peeking over the edge of the bodice. He trailed his gaze over the ribbon that did a very poor job of holding the front closed—one tug and she'd burst out—then he continued on to slide over her cinched waist to the impossibly tight and short lower half of the dress, which didn't even come close to covering her whole ass. She had on a black lace thong, so it definitely looked like she had no panties on at all, followed by fishnets. She had yet to slip on her black heels, which would put her somewhere in the range of Zane's shoulders, but as it was, Zane shifted his incendiary gaze right back up her body, leaving behind a trail of steam that made Cammie feel like the sexiest woman alive.

"I'm not sure you're going to make it through the night with that dress on." Zane did another sweep of her body and she practically melted all over again. He swooped in, hands on her ass, cupping her cheeks, his chest pressed to her tits and hovering his lips over hers. "I hope you're okay with PDL, because I'm not going to be able to help myself."

"PDL?" She gasped as he nipped her bottom lip.

"Public displays of lust," he growled before kissing her so fiercely and thoroughly that when he abruptly stopped, her head had jettisoned into space with her body floating slowly after it.

"Yes. Totally okay with that," she gasped out.

He squeezed her ass cheeks hard before letting go. "We should head to this party before I do something to completely derail our investigation." He opened the door of his cabin then offered his arm for her to take.

She giggled as she slipped her heels on then clasped his arm, her heart nearly bursting from all the adrenaline coursing through her body. She wasn't quite sure when it had happened, but somehow Zane had invaded her completely and she couldn't imagine this vacation slash murder mystery without him.

And she had no idea what she was going to do when it was time to let him go.

* * * *

The Whips and Chains Party was exactly what Cammie expected it to be — chaos wrapped up in leather, PVC, latex and a whole lotta skin. The Sky Deck had been transformed from sun umbrellas and beach vibes to an open-air dungeon, complete with cages for brave souls to dance inside, contortionists and acrobats swinging from black-and-red ribbons, sexy servers covered in body paint and nothing else and pounding music that thudded through Cammie's body. A lot of people were dressed similarly to Cammie and Zane, and a few wore masks, which Cammie realized would make it difficult for them to actually identify Salis among the crowd. Luckily for their investigation, each guest was required to wear a name tag to help with breaking the ice, or so it was explained to them when they were asked to find their own on a table with hundreds of magnetic name tags.

"Miss Sheppard!" A familiar voice pulled Cammie's focus from the growing crowd of dancers to a tall, slim, totally fetished-out version of her steward, Ben. "You look so awesome!! I love that dress on you!"

"Wow, Ben, you look amazing!" Cammie meant it too. Ben was completely transformed from his charming, boyish steward persona into a five-inch heel, flowing purple and blue wig, wild makeup super Queen. He was wearing a snug PVC dress with a chain belt that encircled his waist, neck and wrists, linking them together with enough give to allow him to move while still restricting him to some extent. He couldn't lift his arm completely up to wave, but he could flutter his hand in a gesture that looked like a greeting.

"I didn't think you'd recognize me." He was somewhat out of breath once he finally tottered his way to her. The heels were impressive but gave him height where he hadn't needed it, so instead of simply being tall, he was now towering like a skyscraper over Cammie.

She wouldn't have recognized Ben if she hadn't heard him before she'd seen him. "I didn't know that stewards could moonlight as party Queens."

"We don't, usually. I'm just lucky, I guess." Ben grinned like this was an opportunity of a lifetime. "One of the event crew didn't show, so they asked me if I'd like to join the party and of course I said *yes*! Absolutely *yes*! I've been waiting for a chance to show my stuff to Sherri…er…Ms. Bolt. And I'd do just about anything for her. She's so amazing! I mean, I might have planted the seed already, to anyone who would listen really, that my dream job would be to be part of the event crew—"

"Sorry to interrupt, Ben, but did you say you're filling in for another member of the crew?" Zane stepped forward so he could be part of the conversation. "Great outfit, by the way."

"You, too! Love the kilt." Ben beamed. "And yes, Frankie was a no-show. Probably barfing his guts out below deck. He's a bit of a drinker." Ben covered his mouth and cringed. "Sorry… I shouldn't have told you that."

"I hope he's okay," Cammie said with exaggerated concern. "Do you think he got himself to the infirmary?"

"Frankie? Unlikely, he's probably just sleeping it off in our cabin." A voice crackled through the earpiece Ben was wearing, distracting him from their conversation.

"You bunk with him?" Zane asked once Ben refocused on them.

"Uh, yeah, me, Frankie, Clem and Roberto, the Queens from cabin ten. Woo!" Ben tried to pump his arm but only managed to elbow himself because of the chains. "It was nice chatting with you both, but I have to go! Duty calls!"

"Frankie, Francesco... Same guy, you think?" Cammie watched Ben get swallowed by the crowd. Somehow, even with his towering height, he still managed to disappear.

"Absolutely. I didn't see Salis' name tag on the table, so he's got to be here already. Let's find him before this place fills up, then we can investigation cabin ten, shall we?"

Cammie nodded as Zane took her hand then began to weave them into the crowd of partiers.

The closer they got to the dance floor, which, as it turned out was clear plexiglass on top of the pool, the louder the music thumped. That, with the strobe lights flashing and beams of color shooting across the floor, Cammie felt like she was in a dance club rather than on the deck of a ship. It was nearly all-consuming, and her senses pinged frantically with so much stimulation. She wanted to grab Zane, spin him around and dance her heart out, but she knew that the longer they waited, the more flooded the space would get with bodies and the harder it would be to find Salis.

Even though the Sky Deck was open air and there was a nice breeze coming off the ocean, as they neared the center of the crowd, the body heat was almost stifling and the smell of everyone's various colognes and perfumes a little overwhelming. Not only that but because Cammie was so short, she was having a hard time even seeing the name tags, let alone reading them. So, when Zane finally pulled them free from the dance floor, she knew they had to find a better way to locate Salis.

She pointed to the bar that was a little farther away from the thudding speakers and Zane nodded. By the time they slid themselves onto the bar stools, Cammie was coated in a sheen of sweat. "Whew! That was crazy."

"Yeah, not the best way to find our man." Zane ordered himself a beer and Cammie a soda water. "Maybe if we sit here for a while, he'll come to us."

"Definitely what I was thinking." And a brilliant plan because no less than fifteen minutes later, a crowd of dancers converged on the bar.

Cammie scanned every name tag attached to a dancer that came up to order but didn't see any that even started with an S. Her skirt was riding up and her collar was slick with sweat. She had to move around a bit.

"I'm going to do a quick walk around now that the crowd is here." She wiggled herself off the stool. "Don't disappear or I might never find you."

"No worries." Zane patted her vacated seat. "I'll be right here saving your spot."

She grinned before skirting the outside of the dance floor, trying her best not to be swallowed by the crowd and sucked into the melee, which was quickly becoming more chaotic by the second. *Maybe the crowd isn't all at the bar.*

She maneuvered in between spectators and wove around a few make-out sessions. The heat in the space was a mix between tightly packed bodies and full-blown lust. At one point she had to grab a hold of the bars of one of the dancer cages to yank herself through a full-on orgy.

This idea was possibly a mistake and definitely an ineffective way of finding Salis. *Time to get back to Zane.*

The crowd was so dense that she couldn't really tell what way to go, so she heaved herself up to the cage's platform to get a better look and came face-to-face with Salis himself.

There was no mistaking his identity, even without the name tag. The man was almost identical to the guy she'd seen on the floor of her room — except instead of blue eyes Salis had brown and instead of short hair, Salis' was long and in a ponytail. He grinned at her as he danced, reaching out through the bars to hold her in place as he gyrated in her direction. She was flattered, really, but had no time for his sexual advances, so she pushed herself back in an attempt to slip her foot to the ground. Except, there was no ground within reach and the crowd swept her up as if she wanted to body surf — and she *so* didn't want to do that. Despite her yelp and struggling, hands came up under her, hoisting her into the air then moving her through the crowd like she weighed nothing more than a feather.

She tried to signal that she wanted down but that only made the crowd move her quicker until she was dead center and jostling to the beat of the music. She didn't like this, not one bit. But she also couldn't find a way to let anyone know that. Hands held her hips and legs and arms so she couldn't move to disentangled herself. All she could do was pray that no one dropped her on her head.

Chapter Twelve

Zane had watched Cammie slip through the crowd and had kept her in sight as people parted for her like she was a little goddess moving through her acolytes. He saw her face pop up as she pulled herself onto the platform. Clever strategy to see over the heads of everyone on the dance floor...not so clever if you weren't the type to like body surfing.

He'd watched several people do it before Cammie, climb up onto a cage platform then let the crowd move them from one side of the dance floor to the other like it was some kind of rock concert. He knew the moment Cammie was done for when she teetered backward, a sure signal to the crowd that she wanted to be lifted.

He jumped up from the stool, keeping his eyes on the direction the crowd was moving Cammie, then dove in, pushing his way to meet her so he could somehow get her feet back on the ground. Panic snapped inside his gut, making him more aggressive than he needed to be to cut through the crowd, but he couldn't help it. He had to get to Cammie and rescue her. He knew she'd be freaking the fuck out at having no control over her own movement above the crowd.

He shouted, but the sound disappeared into the loud noise of the music, sucked away as it left his mouth. He craned his neck and shifted up, keeping Cammie in his sights, watching her body bob up, then down, then up again. He adjusted course when he saw the crowd turn her to the left then plowed into the throng once again, growing more and more frantic to reach her.

Just as he made it to Cammie, his hands up to snatch her down, the crowd eased her to her feet, almost like everyone knew he was there for her and that they were meant to be together. She landed softly in front of him, her eyes gleaming, lips curling, and he immediately wrapped his arms around her, inhaling her scent, covering her with his arms to keep anyone else from touching her. He shifted them both backward, out of the densely packed dance floor until it was just him and Cammie and no one else.

She looked up at him, locked in with her eyes but also with her body, her arms around his waist, her body pressed to his like they were glued together.

"You okay?" He had to fight to keep the excessive worry out of his voice.

She nodded then shifted up so she could kiss him. She touched his lips with her soft ones, tenderly at first, almost like a thank you, then turned red hot and full of passion, like she needed to devour him as much as he did her. He lifted her higher so he could kiss her properly and she clawed her fingers through his hair, molding herself to him, her every curve fitting perfectly against his body. He probed her mouth, caressed her tongue and sank into her as deeply as he could, never wanting to let her go again.

They kissed for an eternity — not breathing, not moving — just lips to lips, tongue to tongue, consuming one another at the edge of the dance floor.

She pulled away with a gasp. "Let's get out of here."

Zane nodded, his words all tangled up with his lust. *Fuck finding Salis. Fuck searching for Frankie.* He wanted Cammie right *now.*

She led him around the crowd this time, a longer route but definitely a safer one. Instead of heading for the elevator that would take them to his deck, she detoured.

"Where are we going?" He followed her down a walkway along the side of the atrium.

"Shh-hh." She hushed him but kept going, only pausing long enough to open a door he never would have looked twice at that was nestled inside an alcove.

"Are you sure we're supposed to be here?" It was dark but not in a foreboding way. The muted light was enough to see that she was taking him to a narrow staircase.

"It's a secret deck." She giggled as she tugged him after her. At the top of the stairs there was a plaque that read 'Serenity Deck'. "Not many people know it's even here. I read about it when I was researching reviews about the cruise."

Sure enough, as they stepped out onto the compact deck, they were totally alone. There were two double wide lounge chairs set up and an open balcony that gave an unobstructed view of the brilliant night sky. Zane looked up and around, but they were completely isolated. No one would even know they were up there. There were no windows to even look at the deck from and no other ways onto it. Zane could definitely see why it was a secret hideaway.

Cammie slipped her arms around his waist then tugged him closer. "Let's finish what we started." She tilted her face, her lips begging to be kissed.

There was no way he could resist.

He kissed her as he slid his hands under her dress and cupped her ass. She tugged the rest of his shirt out of his kilt then yanked it open so she could run her fingers over his chest and tease his nipples.

Lust burned a trail down his body and ignited his need to fuck Cammie hard, fast and thoroughly. His cock was like a steel rod, aching to pound her sweet pussy. Luckily, he'd thought ahead and had put a condom in the waist of his kilt. He plucked it out then tossed it to the lounge chair before pulling away from Cammie, his breath ragged and heart pounding.

"Get on the chair, ass up." The words came out guttural and gravelly, but thankfully not desperate sounding, even though that's how he felt.

Desperate to fuck her.

Desperate to keep her.

Cammie didn't have to be told twice. She spun quickly then did as he'd said, hopping onto the lounge chair on her hands and knees, looking so deliciously open to whatever he wanted to do with her.

He moved in behind her and swept his hands over the tight corset binding her waist while grinding his kilt-covered dick against her ass. The faux leather was a thick barrier, taunting him but also giving the right kind of abrasion, pain and pleasure mingling into one. She rocked into him, pushing herself back so he could dry-fuck her, driving himself wild and amping up his need to take her hard.

He reached up, touching the ribbon that held her top together then gave it a tug. The corset blossomed open and her tits sprang free. He cupped both and squeezed, pinching her nipples between his fingers while pushing his aching cock against her fishnet-covered ass.

She picked up the condom and held it out to him. No words were necessary. She needed to be fucked just as much as he needed to fuck her.

Who was he to deny her that?

He unclasped his kilt and let it fall to the deck then snatched the condom. Cammie flipped her skirt up, then tore her tights right down the crack of her ass. Her pale skin shone in the night sky like an actual moon, and all he wanted to do was leave his mark. While he rolled the condom on his dick, he revved up his other hand then gave her a slap that echoed across the open space.

She cried out as she rocked forward, and before she could settle back, he did it again, marking her other cheek with his hand. He used his palm like a paddle, keeping his hand firm and taut as he slapped until her ass cheeks had a rosy glow and radiated heat. She tried to squirm away, but he held her in place as he leaned down to kiss her tender flesh. She moaned and writhed, slipping her fingers to her clit, letting him know that she wouldn't wait for him. He'd punish her for that later, but for now, he yanked her thong out of the way then pinioned her fast and hard, sliding into her tight, wet pussy with a groan.

He slapped her hand away and took over rubbing her clit as he pummeled her from behind. He couldn't help but fuck her like a piston, going so fast that his brain barely registered that his climax was already at the brink of explosion. He couldn't dig in deep enough. He couldn't rub her fast enough.

She moved with him, keeping pace with each thrust, pushing back for more, rolling her hips so that his dick got harder and his balls grew tight.

Her scream was husky and ended with a long moan as her pussy spasmed around his cock, squeezing him like a vise until he couldn't hold off. He couldn't keep his climax at bay and bellowed his own release so that it cascaded along with hers.

* * * *

They lay in a tangled heap of arms and legs and sweaty bodies, clothes askew and not a care in the world. The night air was cool but not cold. The smell of the ocean cleared Zane's head and the unbelievable sparkle of the stars above made him grateful for every moment he got to spend with Cammie in his arms, sharing this time with her.

"I found Salis," she said as she traced a pattern over his chest.

"You did?" Zane looked down at her at the same time that she looked up at him. Her eyes were crinkled like she was holding back a giggle and he couldn't help thinking how much he wanted this to last forever.

Which was all wrong for a guy who only wanted a fling.

"He was in the dance cage. I saw him just before the crowd took me." She grinned. "He was pretty good too. Definitely had some moves."

"Definitely not dead then." He nudged her closer.

Cammie snorted a laugh. "Nope. But also definitely not the guy who was on my floor."

"Obviously not, if he was dancing in a cage." He squeezed her as she laughed again. "I suppose we need to figure out a way to get into cabin ten and check if Frankie is there." Because no matter how much he wanted to stay there all night, he knew there was a job to do. Maybe it wasn't the job he'd come on board to tackle, but it was one that needed getting done.

"Yeah, I was thinking about that." She shifted herself up, her tits swaying beautifully, completely distracting him and making him reach out to — "If you do that, we'll never get my plan started."

He was only millimeters away from her nipples. "Hmmm?"

She swatted his hand playfully. "I was thinking that the crew cabins are probably close to empty tonight because of the party. Not only that but there are a dozen more events underway as we speak. I checked the itinerary." She tugged her corset closed, shutting her glorious tits away and, in doing so, snapping him out of his nipple fog. It took her seconds to retie the ribbon that held her top closed.

He pushed back his disappointment. She was right, of course. They had to get back at it.

"So, you think we should sneak down there to see if we can find Frankie?" He had the urge to push back, to convince her to lie there with him all night. He wanted to fuck Cammie again, then sleep under the stars, but he knew she was right. They needed to keep working. Time was not on their side.

"Exactly." She tugged her ripped fishnets off before putting her heels back on. "I think we'll have a better chance of not getting caught if we go right now." She plucked his kilt from the edge of the lounger. "If we run into trouble, we'll just pretend to make out again."

Zane snatched his kilt from her fingers while at the same time trapping her wrist with his other hand. "Pretend, my ass." He yanked her closer then kissed her with everything he had. There was no way he would ever be able to pretend to want this woman. For him, it was full on, one-hundred-percent undeniable attraction. With the way she curled into him, her hands roving his chest, he suspected it was the same for her.

Which meant that they were both in a butt-load of trouble, because Zane knew it was going to take everything in his power to give her up and walk away. They might have started something that was only going to end up fucking with his head and maybe, no, *definitely*, fuck with his heart.

What was worse than being alone was knowing that there was someone out there who could shine a light in the darkness and make a man feel whole again. He hadn't laughed so much in decades — maybe ever — and being with Cammie made him feel weightless. Knowing that there was someone out there who Zane wanted to be with but who was not available was definitely going to fuck him up and yet, nothing would stop him from being with Cammie now, not while he could, not while she was available to him, while she wanted him, too.

Chapter Thirteen

It wasn't hard to sneak below deck. There was surprisingly very little security around, which confirmed to Cammie that she'd been right about how busy the night was for staff and crew. When she'd checked the itinerary, she'd seen a packed schedule and had known it would come with a lot of chaos to manage.

The halls were narrower in the crew quarters, which made Cammie want to move quickly to get to cabin ten. Being in the cramped space had her nerves all jittery and she expected to run into someone who would question why they were there. But after a couple of wrong turns, they ended up at Ben's cabin door without being stopped by anyone. Cammie tested the knob, twisting it to the right, only to find that the door was locked.

Because of course it was.

"You don't happen to know how to pick locks, do you?" She flashed a quirked eyebrow Zane's way.

"I do, but that's not going to work here." He motioned toward the knob. "There's no visible locking mechanism."

She looked again and swore. "Right, so what do we do?"

"If I had something to leverage, I could knock out the pins in the hinges and we could get in that way." Zane inspected the door. "But that would make some noise."

The door swung open, and Cammie jumped, hand to mouth, holding back a scream.

"Can I help you?" A young man with white bleached hair, dark roots and deep circles under his eyes stood in front of them. "You're not supposed to be down here."

"Yes, we know," Cammie said as she fought to regain her composure. Her mind spun through the excuses she could make in the moment, but they all sounded ridiculous. "We were just..."

Zane picked up what she started. "Ben sent us down here to grab his—"

"Spirit gum!" Cammie finished. "For his falsies." She fluttered her eyelashes. "They're not staying put with all the sweat."

The guy blocking the door took a few seconds to consider the excuse then shrugged. "It's probably in his closet. He keeps all his makeup in there."

Cammie let her breath out slowly as she stepped into the cramped cabin. Zane held the door open and stayed put in the doorway, which was for the best since there didn't seem to be enough space for three adult bodies moving around. "Are you Frankie?"

She knew the guy who flopped himself on the bottom bunk of one of four beds wasn't Frankie, but out of all the names Ben had thrown out earlier, she could only remember the one she was looking for.

"Nah, I'm Clem." He knocked on the roof of his bunk. "Frankie's bed is here, not that he uses it very much."

Ben's closet had his name on it and Cammie found the spirit gum pretty quickly but she pretended to be searching so she could keep Clem talking.

"Oh, Frankie's not much of a sleeper?" Cammie said as she parted a couple of hangers so she could peek deeper into the closet. Ben had a pink sequined dress hanging at the back that would look killer on him.

"Not in this room, anyway." Clem grunted as he lay back on some propped-up pillows. "He's usually partying with the girls."

"The crew?" Zane asked. "Definitely can't blame him there. Lots of reason to party with those beauties."

Clem made a disgusting noise of agreement with Zane. "Damn straight."

"Ben said that you guys like to party in here." Cammie held the spirit gum bottle up to show Clem before closing the closet door.

"That's more Frankie's thing. When he's around, we do party, otherwise it's pretty boring." Clem yawned. "Better for me that Frankie isn't around, though. I only get six hours off to sleep and eat tonight before my next shift."

"Ben said he was covering Frankie's shift at the Whips and Chains Party." Zane leaned against the door, holding it open with his body. "Seems like the guy does too much partying, not enough working."

Chem snorted. "Yeah, right? Probably off with Sherri or something."

"Sherri the event director?" Cammie's mouth dropped open. It was top-tier inappropriate for an event manager to fool around with the staff.

"Yeah, they have a thing—or did on the last trip anyway. He spent a lot of time in her cabin. She's got a private one because she's so important." Chem spat the last words out like they tasted awful. "Too stupid to realize that Frankie's only using her for the luxury."

"Sorry for barging in on you," Cammie said as she moved the short distance to the door. "The way Ben made it sound, we were expecting a raging party down here. Didn't think we'd be interrupting anyone's sleep."

"No problem." Clem waved them off. "I wasn't asleep. Just enjoying the quiet."

"Okay, well, have a good night," Cammie said.

"Yeah, thanks." The door was almost completely closed when Clem called out. "Hey, when you see Ben, can you tell him not to send guests to get shit for him? No offense, but passengers really shouldn't be coming down here."

"We will. Sorry for bothering you." Cammie let the door close. "This is going to get back to Ben."

"Yeah, but now we know where to find Frankie." Zane was already moving down the hall toward the elevator.

"Sherri's cabin," Cammie said. "How are we going to get in there?"

"We're not," Zane said. "We're going to check the surveillance on her deck."

"You have access to all the cameras?" Cammie was sure that Zane had never mentioned that before.

"I do, and, if we're lucky, the staff deck camera will still be working." Zane hit the up button. "If Frankie is in Sherri's room, we'll see him coming and going as long as there's a recording."

"And if there is a camera and we don't see him?" The elevator arrived and Cammie stepped on.

"Then we know who we need to talk to next."

* * * *

Cammie watched Zane, hunched over and madly typing, his kilt spread out around him. All she wanted to do was curl up on his lap and kiss his neck…then his chest…then lower.

"I'm backtracking to prior to departure," he said, oblivious to her lusty thoughts. "The security feed on Sherri's deck is working."

"It's weird how some decks have cameras and some don't." Cammie peered over Zane's shoulder at the various camera feeds. "I wonder why?"

"Not sure, but it's definitely going in my report to my boss." He quirked an eyebrow over his shoulder. "There's something fishy about Chief Ross. His lie about watching footage from your deck was either due to his arrogance or his stupidity. He knows there's no camera and doesn't care if we find out, or he doesn't know and isn't really the chief of anything."

"I'd vote a little bit of both." Cammie didn't like Ross, not only because he'd all but scoffed at her when she'd reported a body on her floor but also because it wasn't enough for him to shove her story aside. He had to insinuate that she had lost her mind as well. He'd even called her hysterical at one point. "Someone probably removed the camera on my deck."

"Not a job that can be done without security knowing." Zane clicked a few more keys. "I'd love to talk to Ross, figure out how deep his ignorance or duplicity runs, but my hands are tied. I'm not supposed to be here."

"It'd be different if you were a detective, I guess." She watched the screen as Zane zeroed in on one camera's feed.

"Yeah, I'm more like an undercover agent. I can't let anyone know I'm investigating." Zane pointed at his computer. "There's Frankie."

Cammie leaned closer, taking in Zane's musky scent, battling the urge to lick his neck. The whole concept of him being undercover, all stealth-like, made her pussy clench. "Yep, that's him." She watched Frankie enter Sherri's cabin, then Zane sped up the recording.

"Three hours later, there he is again." Zane nods as Frankie exists Sherri's room.

"That's only a few hours before I found him on my floor." *Dead.*

Zane zoomed through the video and Frankie never went back to Sherri's room, probably because he wasn't among the living any longer. Sherri, on the other hand, came and went, always in a frenzy, moving quickly and hardly spending any time in her cabin. It was obvious that the woman was dedicated to her job because, as Zane sped through the footage, the longest span of time she stayed alone in her cabin was a few hours.

"So that's that." Zane let out a huff. "We'll need to speak to Sherri. See if she can tell us anything."

"Without her figuring out she's being investigated." Cammie slipped her hands over Zane's shoulders, massaging the tension she saw there.

"Ohhhh, yes, that feels good," he moaned.

She shifted up to her knees so she could really dig into his sore muscles.

"Your hands are magic." He leaned back so she continued her kneading over his chest.

"I bought something else when we were in the fetish store," she purred against his ear.

He straightened his spine. "Tell me more." His chest rumbled with a low groan as she worked a knot.

"How about I show you?" Cammie slipped away before he could object and went straight into the restroom. "Back in a jiff!"

She'd stuffed the outfit, if you could call it that, under the sink before they'd left for the party, and when she pulled it out to look at it again, she had a moment of hesitation. She loved playing dress-up, but this was…well, very daring for her. The mannequin she'd seen it on had been about as curvy as she was, and it had looked so appealing in the store. She held the leather straps and buckles up to the mirror. It was the kind of kink wear that would only take form once it was on her.

What the hell? It wasn't like she was going to disappoint Zane now that she'd teased him.

She quickly stripped then, somehow, remembered how each of the straps were supposed to go. There were chains to attach but she'd let Zane do the honors.

With a deep, steady breath, and her heart in her throat, she flung open the door and tried to keep the grimace off her face.

Would he like it? Would he think it was too much?

"Ho-ly shiiiit!" Zane took her in from head to toe then back again.

The leather outfit had a high collar that was tight against her throat, then straps that went down, parting around her breasts to a corset that cinched her tight enough to make Cammie very aware of each breath she took. There was nothing on the bottom, so she stood there, practically naked — no, *absolutely* naked, but for a few straps and flaps.

"You like it?" Her voice sounded breathy, probably because her lungs were being squeezed inside the corset.

Zane nodded enthusiastically, which dampened any nervousness roiling in her stomach.

"I need some help with the final touches." She held up the nipple clamps that dangled from the collar, then turned to show him the wrist cuffs that would secure her arms behind her back.

The bed squeaked as Zane launched himself from it. He was on her in less than a second, tugging her hands into the cuffs, then latching them tight around her wrists. "Good?"

Cammie bit her lip as she glanced over her shoulder, her range of motion limited by the collar. Zane pulled on the chain that bound her arms to her body, teasing the give, which wasn't much. She slumped into him, her hands just at the right level to rub his cock through the kilt he still wore.

He pressed his lips to her earlobe, teasing the sensitive spot, so tingles rushed over her scalp and down her spine. "You did good, Cammie," he growled. "Safe word?"

She shivered, her legs wobbled, her pussy ached. "Crimson." She wanted his hands on her clit, not on her hips where they teased along the crease of her pelvis.

"The clamps —"

"Are you rushing me, woman?" He swatted her tit hard enough to sting.

"No, Sir." She pressed her palm against the bulge in his kilt.

"Good girl. Crimson is a good choice of word. Your skin will be flushed red when I'm finished with you." He cupped both her breasts, weighting them in his hands before tenderly stroking her nipples until they were pebble-hard and throbbing. He jangled the clamps, letting them bang against one another so they clattered. "These look tight."

He pinched one nipple so hard that she cried out, but before the pain subsided, he attached the clamp and sent the burn deep into her tit. She moaned as her body fought to absorb the shock of such sharp prongs digging into her sensitive nipple. He turned her around, whipping her so quickly that her breast swayed, causing a fresh wave of pain to rocket through her. He latched onto her other nipple with his lips, sucking, licking, soothing one where the other burned like a thousand suns. She closed her eyes and enjoyed the contrast. He blew on her wet nipple, and it tingled pleasantly. As he lulled her with his attention, her shoulders lost their tension, and she let her head fall back. When he stopped licking her with lazy strokes, she wondered why, but only for a second – then she remembered. He clamped the other nipple, the metal teeth biting down hard, but before she could scream through it, he swallowed her mouth with his, taking her sound, her moans, her whimpers into him and devouring her whole.

Her legs couldn't hold her but it didn't matter, because Zane had her. She let him take control. He hoisted her up by the cuffs on her wrists, forcing her back to arch so her breasts pulled taut and her nipples pulsed all over again. She moaned long and low, a deep growl that came from her belly and rolled over her tongue, making her sound like an animal.

"I like the noises you make, Cammie." Zane put her on her knees, then forced her face onto the mattress, turning her head so she could breathe. "I want to hear you when I'm fucking you."

With one hand still yanking her wrists back, he reached around and brushed his other hand against the clamps, pulling a hiss from her lips.

"That's right, Cammie. That's what I want to hear." He pressed her deeper into the bed, forcing her chest down so her tits squished against the soft fabric, a million tiny daggers of sensation against her aching nipples. They burned. *Oh God*, they burned.

"Ohhhh," she moaned.

He nudged her legs apart with his knee and she heard the scrape of the buckle on his kilt as he unlatched it. The kilt fell away with a clatter to the floor. A few more shifts, tugs, then he slipped a silky rope across her shoulders, just above her breasts and another around her corseted torso. He yanked her body upward slightly and her body backward so her tits pulled off the bed by mere centimeters, tweaking her nipples in their clamps and maddening her even more as they scraped along the sheets.

She groaned right from her belly — a tortured sound to match the pain.

"Keep your head down as low as you can, Cammie." His voice, full of warning, let her know that if she didn't heed his words there'd be punishment.

She strained to keep it down and wanted to so badly to press her cheek to the mattress, but the rope tugged her up and back just enough to prevent her from doing that. She had to brace her weight with her knees to keep from swinging forward. Her tits jiggled with every shift she made, sending jolts of fresh agony through her upper body.

"I bought something for you, too." Zane's words were punctuated by a buzz that Cammie knew all too well. "Stopped by Steve Posh's vibrator stand and picked up this beauty." He shifted forward, nudging her ass with his cock as he showed her the dildo. "I thought it would commemorate our trip."

It took Cammie a second to realize that the graphics on the vibrator made it look like a BBQ rib.

"You do like your smoked meat," he said.

Cammie tried to stifle her laugh but just ended up snorting. Her tits jostled anyway, and she moaned through the fresh pain as the clamps seemed to bite down harder on her aching nipples.

Zane smacked her ass with enough force to make her knees skid along the sheets but not enough to take her mind off the clamps.

He slapped her again and again, making the heat rise on one ass cheek while leaving the other alone. With the vibrator still buzzing, he trailed it along her shoulders, sending shivers down her spine. He curled his other hand around to stroke her clit, barely rubbing. She ground down, hoping to get more friction, but he moved with her, keeping his touch teasingly light.

She was so distracted by his finger on her clit that she forgot about the vibrator, which he moved from her shoulders, down her collar, then straight to her tits.

Her nerve endings flared white hot, sparking pain straight to her nipples.

"Oh fuck!" She rocked back, desperate to move away from the vibration, but there was no escape. Zane rolled the vibrator to the clamps, sending a shockwave of agonizing pleasure through her body.

She curled her toes and rocked her hips and Zane delicately tapped at her clit, maddeningly soft and tender.

Her orgasm was miles away, the waves building slowly, steadily, but well out of reach.

"Zane," she moaned.

"That's what I like to hear." He tugged on the rope with one hand while helping her shift farther back on her knees with the other. Then he moved around her suspended body so he was in front of her. "You ready to get fucked?"

Cammie licked her lips and nodded. "Yes, Sir."

His eyes gleamed, along with his grin. His cock was already sheathed with a condom, so when he helped her settle, straddling his hips, he thrust into her, stretching her open, filling her up. The ribbon rope around her body helped steady her movement so she could rock forward, then swing back. She rolled her head, which tightened her collar and pulled her nipples up, but she didn't care. The pain mingled with her desire, and she reveled in it.

"Ride me, baby." Zane placed the dildo at the base of his cock so that each time she rolled forward on his shaft, her clit got a taste of the vibration. It was enough to move her faster, to ride him harder, if only to get more of what she wanted.

She didn't notice Zane reaching for her tits, but suddenly the clamps opened and the raw throbbing shot straight to her pussy. He latched on with his lips, alternating from one bud to the next—sucking, flicking, heightening the burn that cascaded over her nipples and straight to her clit.

"Zane," she screamed, but he didn't stop.

Each roll of her hips flung her cresting orgasm higher and higher until the peak was as tall as a skyscraper. She was so close...so close that she could almost grab hold. She arched into him, nailing the vibrator as she thumped down hard on his shaft, a frenzy of sensation, his lips on her tits, her clit weeping for release, her body primed and ready...to...explode.

Zane gripped her ass and kept her moving, even though her brain had turned to mush and she'd lost control of her body. He rammed his cock deep, forcing her clit to take more and more of the reverberation so her orgasm became an endless loop. His cock seemed as hard as rock, and he bellowed his release, pumping until every last ripple and spasm jolted through her.

Chapter Fourteen

"You two left the party early last night!" Sherri was all sunshine and effervescence which, as far as Zane was concerned, was an absolute crime at nine in the morning. "You missed the best part!"

"Oh, I'm pretty sure we didn't." Zane mustered up a wink for Sherri's benefit. He was nursing a coffee, while Cammie was loading up her plate at the buffet.

"Sherri!" Cammie did a good job matching Sherri's tone and demeanor, especially since he knew that, like him, she was working on only a handful of hours of sleep. "We really enjoyed the Whips and Chains Party last night." Cammie set her plate down, along with one for him, both heaped with so much food that Zane could kiss her.

"I was just saying to Zane that you two left early and missed all the fun stuff." Sherri pouted. "I saw you body surfing, though! Very brave of you!"

"Oh, well, yeah, I can honestly say I've never done that before." Cammie laughed. "I was so impressed with the party. Did you plan it all yourself?"

"Yes, it was all me." Sherri's eyes lit up. "I'm honored by the compliment. A little birdy told me that you work for Sabine Cowan." Her hand fluttered to her chest. "She is my absolute hero."

"I do! And yes, your party — among other things on this cruise — have been totally up to Sabine's standards." Cammie leaned forward. "And adding Ben to your roster as a Queen was a fantastic idea as well. He looked amazing!"

"Ben is a Godsend!" Sherri gushed. "He jumped at the chance to fill in a hole I had in my roster and totally went above and beyond."

"Ben was telling us that Frankie bailed on you. So unprofessional." Cammie *tsked* as she shook her head.

"Yes, it was." Sherri's smile faltered for a millisecond before she covered it up. "But things happen, and I'm always prepared to pivot." Sherri sounded like she was giving an interview, and Zane found himself ping-ponging between her and Cammie, wondering who was more a master of deception. "I hope you two have plans to sign up for some of the amazing events we have happening today!"

"Oh, we definitely do." Cammie speared some eggs from her plate. "Just curious... Do you have to pivot frequently? Do your plans go sideways when it comes to crew bailing? I only ask because Sabine has been toying with the idea of chartering a cruise for her high rollers and —"

"Oh my God! She has? Could you put a word in for me? I'd be so thrilled to help her plan." Sherri seemed to catch herself and quickly reeled back her enthusiasm.

"To answer your question, no, we don't often have staff or crew missing shifts, not unless they get sick, which is rare. Frankie isn't unreliable normally, but he's been distracted recently. I think he might have lost his love of cruise life." Sherri winced. "It happens sometimes. But not to worry, if Sabine charters a fetish cruise with Dark Matter, I'll make sure there are no wayward staff on board."

"Wonderful to hear." Cammie kept her eyes on Sherri, even though her fork was hovering close to her mouth. "And yes, I absolutely will pass your name along to Sabine if she decides to go ahead with her plan."

"Thank you! I should let you eat your food before it gets cold. I'll catch up with you two later!" Sherri spun then beelined for her next targets.

"Thoughts?" Cammie said before finally eating her eggs.

"She's driven." Zane had already consumed half of his plate in the time that Sherri and Cammie had been talking. "Not sure if she'd be driven to murder, though."

"Yeah, she's hardcore into her job, but I seriously don't think she would purposely sabotage her events' success by handicapping herself with a missing crew member. I also don't think she knows where Frankie is." Cammie set her fork down. "And we know he's not in the infirmary or in his own cabin."

"I think it's safe to surmise that he's your dead man." Zane picked up some toast.

"We need to find the body." Cammie sipped her coffee.

Zane sucked back the food in his mouth in a half gasp, half WTF? He started coughing, his eyes leaking as he hacked up the piece of toast that had gone down the wrong way.

Cammie whopped him a few times on the back before handing him his orange juice. "Okay?"

He got himself under control, aware of the fact that most eyes were on him and a server was hovering close, looking ready to deliver some kind of life-saving procedure in case he decided to almost drop dead.

"I'm okay," he wheezed, his hand up to wave the server away. He dropped the toast that was still in his hand then pushed his plate away. He waited until everyone seemed to go back to their own business.

Cammie leaned closer. "Without a body, we won't—"

"We're not hunting for a body," he whisper-growled. "I need to talk to Jasper Haversmith."

"You think Jasper has something to do with this case?" Cammie's whispered words were full of surprise or maybe intrigue. It was hard to tell because she wasn't looking at him and instead was sweeping the crowd of guests seated close to them.

"I think he knows things, and I need to find out what they are." He leveled her with a hard look as she swung her eyes back to him finally. "Promise me you won't go looking for Frankie's body."

Cammie shifted her gaze away for half a second before looking at him again. "I can't prove anything without a body." She rubbed her forehead like he was giving her a headache. "No one even believes that Frankie's body was on the floor of my room—no one except you."

"I know, but the more you bring attention to us, the harder it will be for me to find evidence for *my* case. I'm supposed to be undercover." He reached for Cammie's hand and she let him touch her, but only for a moment before pushing her chair back.

"The easiest way for you to get to Jasper is to go through Bill." She smiled at the server who came to get their empty plates. "Thank you." She got up, looking down at Zane in a classic power move. "I can help you do that."

Zane had to admit that she was right. He had no plan, other than to somehow track Jasper down and weasel his way into a conversation again. "You're willing to help me snag Jasper?" He sensed strings attached.

"I'll get you in with Bill and his son, but you have to agree to help me find Frankie's body." She nailed him with her own version of a hardened stare.

The Dom in him perked up and took notice.

Chapter Fifteen

Cammie had noted that while Zane hadn't made any promises to help her find Frankie's body, he hadn't said no either. She knew where he was coming from. Sniffing around for a dead body was going to bring attention to them eventually, but she hoped he'd learn enough through Jasper to take the chance at exposing himself as a PI. Besides, if they did it right, they might just get away with snooping and not being caught.

Zane had waffled on the commitment, but she had time to convince him — something she was beginning to realize applied to their relationship status as well.

She'd come onto the cruise looking for a hookup and nothing else but had waltzed right into the arms of an amazing guy who'd ticked all her 'yes' buttons — repeatedly and with utmost satisfaction. The chaos he tended to bring, the spontaneity, was growing on her, too. She wanted to see where things would go between them back in the real world.

"Bill and his posse will be at the Gentlemen's Club." Okay, it wasn't called a Gentlemen's Club per se but it might as well have been called that. When Zane screwed up his face, she added, "The Burlesque Room."

Understanding dawned and Zane nodded. "Good thinking. No need to register for that one." Which meant he wouldn't have found it in any of his algorithms. "They open the bar in that room early, don't they?"

"Yes, breakfast mimosas on tap, according to the website, and if I know men like Bill—which I do—he'll be there first thing, while the girls are fresh." She rolled her eyes.

The dancers rotated in and out to keep them from getting too exhausted. They were supreme athletes, but burlesque was demanding and, with a cruise like this, the audience would want big and bold. Cammie had read on the site that they not only performed acrobatics but they used ribbons and hoops suspended from the ceiling for much of their show. Bill would likely be half in the bag by noon and too drunk to notice the difference from one girl to the next, so he'd never know that the *fresh* girls he was watching were different throughout the day. Same thing happened at Kitty Cat events… The men liked to think they had their favorites among the performers but they never could really tell who was who with all the makeup and costumes.

"I say we swoop in there all casual, like we're checking out something new, then cross our fingers that Bill catches sight and does his usual thing," Cammie said.

"I think we can count on him doing his usual thing... 'There's my sweet little honey pot girl'," Zane teased with a southern drawl.

Cammie swatted him but laughed all the same as they made their way down two flights of stairs to the deck that hosted a movie theater, an adult arcade and the Burlesque Room, which was really more of a games' room with dancers.

The lighting was dimmed so it looked like it was the middle of the night rather than first thing in the morning. The music was classic burlesque — a gravelly female singer belted out an updated version of *I Put a Spell on You* on the stage, surrounded by dancers, which only added to the dark and mysterious atmosphere of the space. Like everywhere on the ship, the room was 'decked out to the tits', as Sabine would say. There was an over-the-top feel about the decor — gilded everything — seriously making it look like someone had puked gold leaf onto anything that was stationary. Even the chairs, which were a deep, plush red velvet, had gold brushed along the arms and frames. There was a large oak wood bar along the back wall, with two bartenders, who were dressed as fetishized versions of their Wild West counterparts. Their chests were bared and nipples clamped, ball gags making sure they couldn't speak, which was an interesting touch, and chaps with strategically placed thongs that looked more like leather dick wraps than anything else.

Zane's eyes widened more and more as he took in the chaos, and Cammie had to wonder if the shenanigans in the room were pushing any of his boundaries because, so far, she hadn't found anything that bothered him when it came to sex, sexual expression or fetishes in general.

One of the dancers swung lazily on a thin metal hoop. Her ass precariously balanced so that her legs were crossed like she was riding a horse side-saddle. She wore nothing but body paint and, as Zane got within range, she swooped down, hanging from her knees and whooshed over the top of his head, blowing him a kiss as she passed by.

Zane ducked, checked to make sure she wasn't on her way back to buzz him a second time, then straightened. "This is…um…interesting."

The dancer swept by them again, this time, spread out like a star, her hands holding the top of the hoop and her feet on the bottom as she began to twirl herself around like a spinning top. Cammie could only imagine what fortitude it took not to barf all over the crowd below and thanked the steel stomach of every one of the acrobats and dancers who were blissfully doing their thing without losing their breakfasts. She had mad respect for their skills. *Mad* respect.

Another dancer was rolling and unrolling herself from ribbons that were anchored to the ceiling. She flipped her way almost to the top of one of the tables, making the guests all gasp, before hoisting herself elegantly back up again.

Cammie caught sight of Bill Haversmith before he caught sight of her, so for a moment—and it was truly only a moment—she got to watch him without him doing his usual song and dance for her. He was still putting on a show, his arms flailing, voice booming almost louder than the music, face red and drink sloshing, but it was the expression on the faces of those he was supposedly entertaining that was the true window. Of the members at his table, only two were people she recognized—his son Jasper and his pal

Elm—but every one of the people keeping Bill company were looking at him with open mockery. And he didn't see it. Or if he did, he didn't care. It made Cammie feel bad to witness such disdain as clear as day on every expression, not just from Bill's son, but from all his supposed friends. Bill was a leech and a nuisance, but her empathy button had always been sensitive when it came to the underdog. Not that a millionaire sexist man was really ever an underdog, but still, it tugged at Cammie's heartstrings to see such little respect flashing Bill's way.

"Why, look who it is, my delectable cookie, Cammie!" Bill pushed his chair back and waved Cammie and Zane over "You two are just inseparable, aren't you? Seems like I can't catch a break where this little morsel of sexy is concerned. I'd sure love to have a moment or two alone with you, sweet girl."

Cammie's empathy bubble popped, spattering to the floor like gunk.

"I'm afraid that's not up to me," Zane said. "Cammie does what Cammie wants."

Bill laughed in his booming way then motioned to the chairs. "Join us!"

"Actually, Zane, didn't you say you were dying to play pool?" She pointed to the arched doorway off to the side where a pair of pool tables sat. She scanned the crowd at Bill's table. "Jasper, do you play? Zane would really love a game or two if you do."

"I sure do!" Jasper all but jumped at the chance to leave the table, just as Cammie suspected he would.

Zane gave her a subtle nod before heading off with Jasper.

Cammie took the seat he vacated, which happened to be right next to Bill. "There you go, Bill. You've got me all to yourself."

"Well, not quite, but I'll take it." He waved a server over. "Drink for you, Cammie?"

"I'll have a soda water."

"Ach, still on the water, eh? Well, make sure you put a little lime in there for Cammie here, would ya?" He nudged her. "You hungry?"

"No, thanks, we just had a big breakfast."

"Well, everyone, this is Cammie Sheppard. She works for none other than Cowan Enterprises, right hand to Sabine Cowan herself." A low murmur that seemed like appreciation passed along the table. Cammie could have argued with him about the right-hand part but she knew it wouldn't matter. Bill had made up his own story about her. "Cammie, you know Elm, and some of these folks were at our dinner the other night. If they're worth their salt, they'll introduce themselves to you on their time. This is *my* time, and I have something I want to show you." Bill pushed his chair back then stood, hand out. "Come with me."

She looked around the table but everyone seemed suddenly preoccupied by their own conversations, so she put her hand in Bill's then let him hoist her to her feet.

She saw Zane setting up the pool balls on the table, his mouth moving, followed by Jasper throwing his head back with laughter.

Bill guided her to a smallish lounge area next to the bar. It was a cozy space with four leather recliners and a glass table at the center. "Now, don't you think this would be a good place for a massage area?"

Cammie wasn't sure why Bill wanted or needed her opinion, but she had to agree. The space was just the right kind of secluded while at the same time being tantalizingly public. "A massage area, sure, or acupuncture. Wax play could work here too." Some of the Kitty Clubs had areas like this that catered to the members who loved to stay in the thick of the action, watching everything going on—girls dancing, conversations happening—while having their own physical needs met. Their own less sexual needs met, that was.

"I know this is your realm of expertise, so I thought I'd ask." Bill tugged on a thick rope and a curtain Cammie hadn't noticed before closed behind her. "And it can become completely private with a little tug."

Cammie had a moment of panic. Her hackles rose and goosebumps prickled along her skin. She didn't like being in an enclosed space with Bill, even if it was only a curtain separating her from everyone else. She centered herself, positioning her body just in case she needed to arm bar Bill into submission. "Seems perfect for a special guest."

"Right?" Bill swept the curtain open again then hooked it back in place. "That's what I keep telling Captain Evans. There are missed opportunities all over the place on this ship. With the right kind of investment, he could turn this place to gold. He should be thinking about hiring someone like you, as a consultant, to fix this place up."

"That's flattering, Bill, but I'm pretty sure my boss wouldn't think too kindly on me moonlighting." She relaxed her stance, realizing that she'd been overreacting to Bill as a threat.

"You could use it as leverage." He motioned her out of the space. "Get a pay bump. Let your boss know that you have transferable skills."

If Cammie didn't know any better, she would have thought Bill was trying to headhunt her away from Sabine. "Oh, she knows my value, and I'm paid very well."

"I'm sure you are, sweetheart." Bill patted her shoulder and she had to give him credit for not going for her ass instead, because she definitely would have put him in a chokehold. "Just so you know, I'd totally be interested in a little wax play with you. I bet you're really good with your little hands. You could probably massage all my kinks out."

Cammie laughed and shook her head. "You're completely incorrigible." *And disgusting.*

"You say that like it's a bad thing." He grinned. "Just remember... I have more money than God and I'm willing to spend it on a pretty little lady like you."

"I'm flattered, truly." Cammie tried not to roll her eyes. "But I'm just not that kind of girl."

"Fair enough!" Bill held his hands up like he was finally starting to understand that she was off limits. She knew it wouldn't last, but she was hopeful for a reprieve that might give Zane enough time to work his PI magic on Jasper.

On their way back to the table, Cammie caught sight of Ben and waved, but he was moving like his ass was on fire, skimming along the edge of the room before disappearing behind a curtain that presumably went backstage.

Jasper was hovering over her seat at the table. "Forgot my cigarettes." He waved the pack in her direction then snatched a lighter from next to her soda water with lime. "Your boyfriend is kicking my ass."

Boyfriend. Huh.

Now that's a word to get stuck on, isn't it? She contemplated Jasper as he walked back to the pool room, her eyes drifting to Zane as he racked the balls once again. *Boyfriend. Hmmm?* She didn't hate the sound of that.

"Shit!" Bill knocked himself so hard against the table that her glass almost toppled over, the water sloshing everywhere. She caught it in time to stop a total mess. "Leave that, darling. I'll get you a new one."

Cammie shook her head as she lifted the glass and took a long gulp. "No worries, Bill. This one is fine."

Chapter Sixteen

Even though Zane was playing pool and chatting up Jasper, he was also keeping an eye on Cammie. Not because he didn't think she could handle herself with Bill and his buddies — she was quite capable of putting Bill and anyone else in their place — but because he didn't like the vibe of the Burlesque Room.

There was something off about the space, almost like the crew and staff were all playing too hard at being natural — or maybe that was just him projecting his own insecurities. With his attention split and wandering every time his brain caught on Cammie, he was having a hard time staying focused on Jasper.

All the same, his hackles were up and in between shots, his gaze strayed toward the other side of the room where Cammie was chatting with Bill and the rest of the table.

"It doesn't bother you that my father is all up in your girl's space?" Jasper caught Zane looking at Cammie for the millionth time. "It would bother me."

Zane shook his head then lined up his next shot. "Cammie can handle herself."

"Yeah, that I can see." Jasper whistled when Zane managed to get two balls in two separate pockets with one perfectly aimed tap. "But still, no jealous twinge? My dad is a wealthy man. Cammie might be tempted."

Zane snorted. "No offense to your dad, but I don't think so." Cammie was used to men like Bill, and if she were enamored by wealth, she had enough of it around her when she went to work to have already indulged.

"Yeah, he's a pig." Jasper drained his wine then set his empty glass on the side table. An eagle-eyed server was already making her way toward them with a refill on her tray.

"Well, that's not what I meant but—" Zane took his next shot and missed.

"No, but it's the truth." Jasper snatched the cue ball then lined up his next move. "Which makes me wonder why you guys keep coming around. Good ol' Bill must be annoying you two by now. He annoys the hell outta me." The last few words were uttered under his breath but loud enough for Zane to get the gist.

Zane watched as Cammie and Bill stood from the table then headed toward the back corner of the room. "We just keep running into him." Zane moved around the table, mostly to keep an eye on where Cammie and Bill were headed while at the same time feigning interest in Jasper.

"That's tragic." Jasper sunk the next three balls in quick succession. "Dad's just showing her the private area to get her opinion. No need to worry. He might be a pig, but he really is harmless."

Zane snapped his attention back to Jasper, slightly annoyed with himself that he'd been caught staring again. "I guess I am a little jealous after all," he lied. No matter what Jasper said, Zane would be keeping an eye on any woman Bill led to a secluded place. "Why does he want Cammie's opinion on the private area?"

"Oh, because the old man is insane." Jasper sunk the eight ball and won the game. "Dad has suddenly decided that instead of a takeover, he wants to revitalize the cruise line. I guess the captain got to him and somehow convinced him to invest instead of dismantle. Apparently, that's why he dragged Elm and the board here. The old kook has it in his head that he can spiffy the place up with more opportunities for sex or play or something equally disgusting coming from a man like him. He wanted to see what Cammie thought about his idea for that space back there—massage or wax or something." He patted his pockets then swore. "I left my smokes at the table."

Zane watched Jasper walk off in search of his cigarettes then noticed that Cammie and Bill were already on their way back to the table as well. Cammie was smiling, so Zane guessed that nothing too obnoxious had happened in the private area. She was fine, and Zane needed to chill out. She had a brown belt in Jujitsu, so she could take Bill and anyone else who bothered her to the floor in a heartbeat. Zane was obviously being a little too paranoid about what he was sensing in the room and a little too invested in Cammie, if he was going to be honest.

He turned to the pool table and began retrieving all the balls from the pockets.

If Bill had changed his perspective on the fate of the cruise line, Zane needed to find out why. Was there some reason to keep the ships moving? Was Bill in on the laundering scheme maybe? It would have to be something to pique Bill's interest as well as ensure more wealth. Bill hadn't become a millionaire by mistake. The man had made wise investments and business decisions from the time he'd been a young man, according to Zane's research, primarily in hostile takeovers and sell-offs. The change in tune was a signal of something, Zane just wasn't sure what.

"You break, Zane," Jasper said as he returned. "I'm going to finish my smoke."

Zane nodded as he moved to the head of the table. "So, your dad wants to invest, even though the price of scrap metal is through the roof right now?"

"I know, right?" Jasper sighed. "He'd make a killing from the scrap of the fleet of ships, and he's got scrappers begging for more metal."

"You think the captain changed his mind?" Zane tried to keep his voice level, like he was interested, but not overly interested, in what Jasper had to say. "You said that the captain had a vested interest in keeping the cruise line going. Seems odd that he'd be so attached to a job."

"The CEO is his brother," Jasper said in between puffs.

Zane missed the shot and barely kept his cue from ripping the felt. *Captain Evans and Cal Underwood are related?* He hadn't come across that little tidbit in his research. "That's handy to have a brother who owns a fleet of ships when you're a trained captain."

"Half-brothers." Jasper put his cigarette out. "Same mom, different dads."

Two more pieces of the puzzle clicked together, but not in a way that made sense to Zane. Was Captain Evans using his brother's cruise line for something nefarious, or was he trying to protect his brother's asset and save the business by convincing Bill to invest?

"Surely the captain knows about the missing money." Zane broke the balls so they scattered all over the table, sinking three right away.

"You kidding? He's the one spearheading an investigation." Jasper leaned on his pool cue. "The man is obsessed with being a captain, and this ship in particular is his pride and joy. Seriously, he'd do anything to keep this arm of his brother's company from tanking." Jasper scoffed. "I think it's just sentimental bullshit. Cal Underwood is a businessman. He shouldn't let family matters get involved in business decisions. He should have sold Dark Matter Cruise Line off years ago."

"You think he's just indulging his brother's love for sailing big boats?" Zane sank two more balls.

Jasper shrugged.

"So, you don't think the captain has anything to do with the missing money?"

"Evans? Nah. He's too much of a boy scout." Jasper tapped his cue on the floor. "You're cleaning up! I'm not even going to get a chance to take a shot, am I?"

Zane chuckled as he lined up another two balls.

"According to my dad, the captain is suspicious of everyone. Thinks that it might be the crew who are up to something, but he can't nail down what's going on." Jasper *tsked* when Zane missed the next shot. "Doesn't help that his Chief of Security is a moron."

Zane snorted.

"Seriously, there isn't a full brain between Ross and Evans." Jasper sunk another ball. "Dad told me that the captain's been cutting corners with security measures to save money."

The missing camera on Cammie's floor must have been a victim of cost savings, along with all the other decks that Zane had noticed didn't have video feeds.

"Now he's got my dad sold on sinking more money into this place when it's hemorrhaging." Jasper shook his head. "I heard the captain even pressured his bro to hire a PI."

Zane froze on reflex but recovered quickly. "Oh yeah?" He tried to sound casual, disinterested even, but the news that it was the captain who'd pushed for bringing in a PI sent Zane reeling. Cal Underwood obviously hadn't been upfront with Zane about having his brother on board as the captain. He also hadn't been upfront about Evans being the one to spearhead the investigation. Was that an effort to keep Zane unbiased or was it an attempt to handicap Zane from the get-go? Or was the captain putting himself up for Zane's scrutiny so that he could be ruled out, because he had nothing to hide? That sounded too calculated for a moron.

It would make way more sense to Zane to have had access to all the captain's knowledge from the second he'd boarded the ship. If the captain wanted Zane blind to keep him from being skewed, then Zane had to wonder why. "Sounds like those old narc stories that used to go around when I was in high school. Everyone was always worried that there was an undercover cop pretending to be a teenager."

"Yeah, right?" Jasper laughed before getting all serious about his next shot. He lined things up then sank the next two balls into pockets. He chalked up his cue before leaning over the table again. "Makes me think that maybe you and Cammie don't just happen to keep running into my father after all." Jasper took out the eight ball. "And maybe there are two investigators on board instead of one."

Chapter Seventeen

For some reason—probably all the salt she'd heaped on her eggs—Cammie was dying of thirst and not only downed her first soda water but a second quickly after. Of course, that meant she had to pee like a racehorse almost instantly, so she excused herself from Bill and his friends then made her way down the darkened corridor to the restrooms. It was cooler in the hallway where the air conditioning didn't have to work as hard to bring the temperature down. Cammie shivered, realizing quite suddenly that she was coated in sweat. All those acrobatics must have been jacking the temperature up in the main room.

The chilly air felt so nice against her hot skin. She'd been having a surprisingly good time chatting with Bill and his friends, laughing at Elm's ridiculous jokes that were often at Bill's expense and overall missing the fact that she'd been overheating while sitting there…which also explained why she'd been so damn thirsty.

After she was done having the most glorious pee of her life, she washed her hands then looked at herself in the mirror. Her cheeks were rosy, making it look like she'd put on way too much blush. Her hair, a tragic victim of humidity, was kinked every which way and fizzled to a curl-destroying degree. She leaned closer then stumbled against the counter, catching herself just in time to keep her head from banging the mirror.

Whoa, I'm dizzy. Her stomach pitched and gurgled. *Maybe I do need something to eat.*

Her pupils were blown out, wide and saucer-like, and her lips were creased, like she was dehydrated, which, of course, was impossible. Her feet were numb, as were her fingers, and she couldn't quite tell if the floor was wobbling or if that was her legs.

She pushed herself back, stumbling again as she got her footing, despite how her head swirled. Her balance was way off as she managed to exit the restroom, bumping and banging her way through the door. Each step was like walking in the deepest mud, slow, unsteady, laborious. She tilted to the side, using the wall to hold her up. Her breath came out in rapid gusts, like she just couldn't get enough air and her heart thundered in her ears. She had to get out of the corridor, but it was so dark that she couldn't figure out which way to go—or maybe her eyesight was narrowing, down to a pinprick of vision.

I've been drugged. The thought seemed too outlandish to believe. She was always so careful with her drinks because she knew all about the perils of sipping something that could be spiked with the odorless, tasteless drugs that were made to incapacitate women.

Another wave of dizziness sent her to her knees. "H-h-help," she croaked.

"Miss Sheppard?" A familiar voice wobbled into her ears, but she couldn't move her head toward the sound. "Oh my God, Miss Sheppard, what's wrong?"

Ben... It was Ben at her side, trying to help her stand.

"I c-c-c-can't—"

"Miss Sheppard, it's okay. I'm going to get help." Ben eased her to the ground so she could lean against the wall. "Medic to the Burlesque Room." He checked her pulse, cool fingers pressed just under her jaw. "You're going to be okay. Just hang on, Miss Sheppard. Help is on the way."

Cammie couldn't even nod. Her head was so heavy that it was hard to hold it up and her eyelids had ten-pound weights pulling them down. She mumbled what she hoped sounded like 'thank you' then gave up the fight.

* * * *

Awareness flashed in Cammie's head like explosions, voices she recognized, words she didn't. She reached for consciousness, desperate to find out what was going on, what was wrong with her, but no matter how hard she fought, she couldn't open her eyes. The explosions had brought pain, so much pain that she couldn't focus on anything else, so she let the pounding headache swallow her down again.

"You're not family, sir. You can't be here."

"I'd like to see you try to move me." Zane's growled words cut through the darkness and pulled Cammie to the surface once again. "You can go ahead and call security. I'm not leaving."

"But, sir—"

"She was drugged." Zane's voice was like a sharp whip. "You don't honestly think I'm going to leave her alone again, do you?"

"Sir—"

"It's okay," Cammie mumbled, her throat raw and dry. "He can stay."

"Cammie, you're awake. Thank fuck." Zane let out a sigh that sounded full of relief.

Cammie eased her eyes open, thankful to find that the room wasn't bright.

"Here." Zane put a water bottle in her hand. "I'm opening it. Can you see?"

She nodded, her eyes focused on Zane's hand turning the lid of the water bottle and the familiar clicking, proof that it had never been opened before. "I was drugged?"

A niggling in her brain told her that she'd already pieced that together before everything went black.

"Rohypnol," Zane confirmed. "Not a ton, but it was enough."

She was slightly upright, so she didn't have far to move to get the bottle to her lips. He helped her all the same, and she managed to take a few sips without spilling any on herself. It washed away the fog in her head and her cotton mouth from hell, so she drank a bit more.

"Miss Sheppard, how are you feeling?" An older woman who fit the image of a nurse to the tee, white lab coat, gray hair pulled into a tight bun, glasses dropping low on her nose, stood on the other side of the bed, her expression full of worry. "Headache?"

"Not right now. Just tired." Cammie drank down half the bottle. "How long have I been out?"

"Four hours." The nurse nodded as she checked the machine next to Cammie's bed. "Your vitals are all good. Do you have pain anywhere else?"

Cammie was sore all over, but it was more of an achy pain rather than a seriously injured pain. "Other than some stiff muscles, no."

"I can give you something for that." The nurse tapped something on the machine.

"I don't take painkillers." And after what had just happened, no way would she ingest another drug, even if it was meant to ease her aches.

The nurse looked down her nose at Cammie, not in a snotty way, more because her glasses were that low on her face. "If you feel up to it, we could have you moved to your suite so you can rest more comfortably."

"She's not going to go—"

"No, it's okay." Cammie put her hand on Zane's arm. "I'd like to go to my cabin."

Even though she hadn't spent one night there, Cammie knew she would be more comfortable in her own space right now. She needed time to think. Time to deal with the fact that someone had hurt her. Someone had abused her safety and her trust. Not that she'd had a lot of it among the crowd she was with but still, she should have been safe. She tried to convey her need to be alone to Zane but the expression on his face was full of confusion and maybe a little hurt.

"I'll get the wheelchair set up." The nurse left the small space.

"Cammie, I think it would be better—"

"I'm okay, Zane." She cut him off before he could convince her to stay with him. As much as she'd take comfort in his presence, she knew he'd abandon his investigation to take care of her, and she couldn't let that happen. It was obvious that he'd already spent the last four hours next to her bed instead of working their case. "I need you to figure out who did this."

Zane's eyes flashed with what looked like understanding, and she was so very grateful for that.

She drank more water, and with each swallow grew more convinced that this was the right decision. "I need you to find out what's going on." She rubbed her head, trying to collect her thoughts. "I didn't taste anything strange in my soda water, but that had to be what was used to drug me. I didn't eat anything after our breakfast." Her drink had already been delivered to the table by the time she and Bill had returned from the private area, but after that, she hadn't left her seat. "Jasper was near my glass when he came to get his cigarettes and lighter."

She frowned… *Could it have been him?* Or Bill, who had knocked her glass in that moment, as well? Could he have been hiding the fact that he was dropping drugs into her drink? She'd like to think that she would have noticed, but she wasn't exactly on high alert at that point. It was a rookie mistake and so unlike her. Normally she would have ordered something fresh to be delivered while she was sitting there, but Bill had made such a big deal about getting her a fresh soda, and she had felt compelled to brush him off.

"Jasper suspects that we're PIs." Zane brow was so furrowed that the indent looked permanent.

"He does?" she croaked around the lump in her throat. So much for being stealthy. Jasper was definitely at the top of her list of suspects now. "So, it could have been him who slipped something into my drink."

"Him, Bill, Elm, the server, the bartender." Zane ticked the names off his fingers. "Maybe all of them.

Someone drugged you to get you out of the way…to get me out of the way." He curled his hand over hers. "I don't want to leave you alone."

"You have to!" It all made sense to Cammie. She'd been given a drug to incapacitate her because she and Zane had gotten too close to the truth.

"Captain Evans was here to check on you. Chief Ross is investigating." Zane couldn't pull off fake reassurance. He knew as well as she did that the security chief could not be trusted to get to the truth. So far, he'd been negligent in following up on anything that involved Cammie.

"You need to find out what's going on, Zane. *You* do." She flipped her hand over so she could entwin her fingers with his. "I'll be okay. I'll have my phone. I'll call you if anything happens."

"Miss Sheppard, I'm so happy to see you awake!" Ben came into the room with a wheelchair. "I was so worried about you." He flipped his hair out of his eyes.

"Thanks for helping me, Ben." Cammie tried for a smile, but even moving her face hurt her muscles. "You were there at the moment I needed you."

"Oh, gosh, right place, right time." He waved his hand. "I'm just happy that I could help."

"Ben is going to take you to your room if that's okay, Miss Sheppard." The nurse lowered the side rail of her bed. "I'll come up to check on you in a few hours."

Zane helped her out of the bed, then carried her effortlessly to the wheelchair. "You're sure?" He asked as he leaned into her. "You don't want me to come?"

Cammie shook her head. "I'm okay. Promise."

"I'll take care of her, Mr. Roberts." Ben put his hand on her shoulder, and she reached up to pat him there.

"All she has to do is pick up her phone and I'll be in her room within seconds."

"I'm good." And she was. She just needed to sleep a little bit more.

Zane looked from Ben to Cammie, his expression full of indecision, but then something seemed to click and he squared his shoulders. "You call me if you need anything."

Cammie nodded then motioned for Ben to get them moving. The last thing she saw before the elevator doors closed was Zane putting his phone to his ear as he darted for the stairs.

* * * *

"There you go, Miss Sheppard. All settled in." Ben was in the process of tucking the sheets around her when she'd finally had enough of his nursing.

"Thank you, Ben, but I think I'm okay. There's no need to tuck me in." She tried to soften her words with a smile, but Ben got flustered anyway.

"Oh gosh, I'm sorry! Overdoing it, as usual." He took a few steps back, his eyes scanning like he was trying to figure out what else he could do to make her comfortable.

"I'm good, really. I just need a bit of sleep." Which wasn't a lie. Now that she was in her bed, she wanted nothing more than to sink down into the pillows, nestled under the comforter and sleep the next few hours away.

"I'll be in the hall if you need me. Just shout, okay?" He twisted his hands together as he took a few steps backward. "Oh, and I snagged you a couple of ice cream bars, just in case you wanted something cold.

You were so hot when I found you. I just thought maybe you'd like something to keep you cool." He winced. "I don't mean to baby you. It's just—"

"Thank you, Ben. That was very thoughtful. I love ice cream bars." This time her smile did the trick and Ben relaxed.

"Oh good, I wasn't sure, but I thought it might be something you'd like." He laughed a little. "I had to sneak into the big walk-in freezer in the galley to get these. They're special. Captain's favorites. Really expensive." He winked. "I hate going into that dungeon. It's so damn cold, but you're worth it."

"I appreciate it, Ben, really. You're special, too." Cammie couldn't help a yawn that nearly split her head in two.

"My pleasure as always, Miss Sheppard." Ben opened the door. "Remember… Shout if you need me."

"Ben, I think you can call me Cammie at this point. No need to be so formal." She yawned again, her eyelids fluttering closed on their own.

"Okay, Cammie, sleep well."

She barely heard the click of the door closing before she was swallowed by sleep again.

"I had to sneak into the big walk-in freezer in the galley to get these ones. I hate going into that dungeon. It's so damn cold…"

Chapter Eighteen

Zane had one destination in mind as he left Cammie in the infirmary, the captain's office, but first he wanted confirmation from Cal Underwood himself that his brother wasn't under suspicion.

"Tell me you've figured out where my money is." Cal started every conversation without preamble and Zane liked that about him. Straight to the point. No unnecessary chitchat.

"Not before you tell me if I can trust your brother." Zane took two steps at a time to get to the atrium where reception was much better for an overseas call.

"My brother was the one who raised the alarm. You can trust him." Cal sounded amused, like Zane had passed some kind of test.

That pissed Zane off.

"My girlfri — my *good* friend has been hurt as a result of being tangled up in this. It would have been good to know that your brother was the captain and that I could count on him as an ally."

"And how did your good friend get tangled up in your case, Mr. Roberts, if you didn't invite her in?" Cal cleared his throat. "Don't think I haven't been appraised of your progress. From my viewpoint, I'd say Miss Sheppard knew what she was getting herself into when she joined forces with you."

Zane bristled but couldn't deny what Cal was saying. It had been Zane who'd agreed to let Cammie into his world. Sure, she'd been insistent, and yes, she had reason to want to investigate after finding a dead man on the floor of her cabin, but ultimately, Zane could have said no. He could have set aside his personal interest in Cammie and kept her out of the loop.

"I'll take your silence as agreement. I am sorry that Miss Sheppard was hurt. I have been told that she's fine now and recovering in her cabin. I have a great deal of respect for her employer, Sabine Cowan, and wouldn't want anything to happen to someone Sabine values."

Zane took those words to mean that Cal was intimidated by Sabine Cowan and wouldn't want to piss her off. "I need to drop the undercover shit and hit this straight on, and I need Captain Evans to back me."

"Do you have a lead that connects to the case I hired you to investigate or are you seeking retribution for your girlfriend?"

"They're one in the same," Zane growled. He wanted to start with Jasper and Bill first, because his gut was telling him that the truth lay nestled in those two, even if they weren't directly responsible for what had happened to Cammie.

Cal let the silence hang for a long minute. "The captain is expecting you." Then he hung up.

To be honest, Zane would have gone to the captain anyway, even without Cal's blessing, but this made things easier.

"You look like a man on a mission." Elm Stone was lounging in a chair on the Sky Deck as Zane beelined through. "How's Cammie? Doing okay, I hope."

"She's resting." Zane shielded his eyes from the sun so he could see Elm, who was glistening with some kind of tanning oil. It was not a good look. "Do you know where I can find Bill and Jasper?"

"Yes, sir, they're speaking with Chief Ross." Elm grabbed his shirt from the arm of his chair. "In fact, I'm headed to the Security Deck myself. I assume you are too. We can't have young ladies getting drugged, no sir."

Zane frowned. He needed to speak with the security chief as well, and now that Cal was on board with Zane's plan, he assumed the captain would be appraised by his brother, which would clear the way for Zane to fill Ross in now instead of later. Plus, he wanted to hear whatever Jasper and Bill had to say. The captain would have to wait.

Elm slipped his shirt over his arms but didn't bother to button it up. "Lead the way, Mr. Zane. I'm right behind you. You been doing this long, Mr. Zane?" Elm was in front now that they were on the elevator, his back to Zane so he couldn't see his face.

"What's that?" Not for the first time, Zane wished he had a weapon with him. The hair on the back of his neck had been at attention with each step he'd taken toward the security meeting.

"Oh, come now," Elm said with a snort as he looked over his shoulder. "Investigative work."

Zane revved up, ready to play the game all over again when he remembered that he didn't need to keep his identity a secret anymore. "A year, give or take."

Elm cocked an eyebrow over his shoulder. "Not long then."

"Solid track record," Zane countered. Which was not really the truth. He had no idea why Cal had hired him out of so many more experienced investigators available.

"Not much of a game face, though." Elm's grin should have been disarming, but for the first time since he'd met the man, Zane saw it in a different way.

"Excuse me?" Zane crossed his arms and widened his stance.

"You came barreling out to the Sky Deck, ready to bust some skulls." He tapped his head. "I knew before you asked where Bill and Jasper were that you'd be stirring up some trouble for me. You and your sweetheart, Cammie, just kept showing up wherever Bill was, and I couldn't make sense of it. Then you started asking questions you shouldn't have been asking and I knew that you suspected Haversmith of something. Taking him down would mean taking me down, and I can't have that, no sir."

Everything clicked into place in that moment. "You're the one siphoning money, aren't you?" Elm was a board member of Bill's company. He had a vested interest in making sure Bill didn't make bad business decisions. He'd traveled with Bill on the first cruise and this one only...why? Because he'd set something up on the first cruise and now Bill was threatening to shut it down with his change in heart about the cruise line takeover? Or something else?

Elm hit the red button and the elevator slowed to a stop. "Siphoning isn't exactly right."

"You're skimming off the top." Zane lowered his arms then shifted his stance again, ready for a strike to come.

"I'm collecting insurance." Elm spread his hands and took a step toward Zane.

"Stay right there." Zane lifted his fists. If he had to, he'd knock Elm's head off.

"Whoa, whoa! I'm not looking for a fight, just a compromise." Elm held his hands up. "A deal between two gentlemen."

"I'm not interested in deals." Zane slid to the side of the car, trying to figure out the best angle to take Elm down.

"Oh, ho! You're not interested in money?" Elm shook his head. "Hear me out, son. I can make you a millionaire." Elm hit another button for the floor just under the Security Deck. "Let's have a drink, and I'll answer your questions." The elevator lurched and Elm frowned at the stop button like it was misbehaving.

"I told you that I'm not interested." He dove for Elm's waist, but his hands slipped along his skin because of the tanning oil, and he crashed headfirst into his gut. They both barreled into the side of the car.

Elm managed to get in a weak uppercut to Zane's jaw, enough to snap his head back with a crunch.

Zane shook it off, then moved to strike again, but Elm cocked him in the temple with his elbow then in the gut with his knee. Zane dropped like a bag of rocks. Black spots spiraled across his vision. He curled in on himself, gasping for breath from a hit to the solar plexus. His diaphragm spasmed as he tried to suck in more air.

"Now, son, it didn't need to come to that." Elm got to his knees, huffing and puffing his way to his feet. "I'm an opportunity man." He brushed dirt from his clothes while Zane desperately tried to clear his head and fill his lungs. "When Bill first brought me on this kink cruise, I saw an opportunity to clean some money."

Laundering, just as Zane had suspected.

"My people collected a fee that maybe cut into the cruise line's profits." Elm shrugged. "But what did I care? As long as my money was coming in clean and whole? Let them take what they thought was fair. The kink cruise industry is too niche to keep afloat anyway, and Bill was planning a hostile takeover, so we'd scrap the ships in the end and cover up my dirty deeds." He wiped his hand over his brow. "Then Bill started to invest money on the sly." He brushed his fingers through his hair. "His own money!" Elm hit the stop button and the elevator began to climb again. "Well, I couldn't let my friend lose his own money on a failing cruise line, now could I?"

Zane pushed himself to his knees, finally able to get air into his lungs but Elm was on him with a quick knee strike to the side of the face that sent him reeling back so his head cracked against the metal handrail. It was a million-dollar hit, striking him in exactly the same place as his last head injury. He not only saw stars, but he saw an entire black hole spinning to the point of nausea.

"I suggest you stay down, boy." Elm kicked him in the ribs—not hard enough to crack any but hard enough to put Zane on his back. "Then I found out that Bill wanted to buy the company! Buy it to revitalize it! What the hell? I was sure the man had lost his mind.

This company is ripe for a takeover and dismantling. A floating fortune in scrap metal."

Zane's brain was scrambled. Elm's words echoed too loud then too soft in his head. A thousand bees buzzed in his ears.

Elm reached down and scooped Zane up under the arm like he weighed nothing at all, forcing him to his unsteady feet. "But Bill's been my friend since we were kids, so what's a guy supposed to do?"

The doors slid open. Zane tried to straighten his spine, but his gut screamed from Elm's sucker punch and his head spun like the earth was rotating off its axis.

"I had to tie up some lose ends here. Let my people know that the game is over." Elm heaved Zane over the threshold and started down the hall. "But Frankie had gotten greedy." He slipped his key card out of his pocket. "So, I had to take care of that."

Zane's head stopped twirling long enough for him to realize what floor they were on.

"Poison is women's work. Not my style but definitely less to clean up." Elm pushed the door open. "Just bad luck your girl stumbled on his body in her room. That dumbass Ben panicked or some shit and hauled Frankie's body in there while he figured out what to do with him. Stuck that greedy bastard in the freezer for safe keeping, which wasn't the worst idea in the world."

He shoved Zane into the room then let the door close behind them. Zane crumbled to the floor, his head blazing as if Elm had nailed him with a spike rather than a handrail.

"Darlin', you in here?" Elm used his shirt to wipe sweat from his brow.

The restroom door swung open. Sherri stood there with a toothbrush in her hand and her mouth full of foam. "Daddy! What are you doing in here with him?"

Chapter Nineteen

Cammie passed out thinking about Ben's words and woke up thinking about them too. She absolutely needed to get herself into the freezer. What better place to hide a body than there? And according to her quick research, the freezer on board a cruise ship like this was deep and had many places that would work to keep a body hidden, especially if no one was looking for one.

Her main problem was Ben, who had said that he'd be acting as her personal bodyguard outside her door while she slept. Now that she had, she was back to one hundred percent, her head clear, body strong, no more aches and pains. Even the nurse, who'd just been in to check her vitals, had confirmed that she was good to go. The nurse likely meant good to go to the Sky Deck, or to the restaurant, not good to go hunt down a dead man.

But, whatever... Hunting down a dead body was what Cammie needed to do. And she needed to do it *now*, before Zane came to talk her out of it.

She picked up her cabin phone and, sure enough, Ben answered before it could even ring. "Miss Sheppard, what can I do for you?"

She could hear him on the other side of the door. "Cammie, and please, come in."

Seconds later, Ben popped his head into her cabin, all bright eyed and beaming. "It's so good to see you up. You look so much better, Cammie!"

"Thank you, Ben. I feel so much better. But I'm hungry! Famished!"

Ben entered the room fully. "What can I get you?" He tapped his earpiece. "I can order you anything you like and have it brought up in no time."

"That's really amazing of you." Cammie winced. "But I was hoping you'd personally supervise my food...you know...because of what happened."

Ben's eyes widened. "Gosh, of course, Cammie, of course! Duh! I'll oversee every step of your food preparation, and I'll deliver it myself."

Cammie smiled. "That's so thoughtful of you."

"What are you hungry for? Soup? Something light?" Ben motioned to the side table. "There's a menu —"

"Soup sounds wonderful." Cammie sighed. "Better to start with something light."

"I'll bring you some fresh bread too, with whipped butter. I love that stuff. I could eat it by the bucketful." Ben was already at the door. "I can get that straight from the galley, so it won't take long to get it ready — maybe enough time for a shower if you feel like it."

Crap! She needed Ben to be busy for long enough for her to get to the freezer without him discovering her gone, and she needed Ben to not be in the galley, which was the only way to get to the freezer. "Actually, now that you mention bread, I think I'd like some ribs from the Smokin' Joe's Bistro, with some of their amazing potato wedges." She rubbed her belly. "And maybe some wings too."

"Okay!" Ben grinned. "That sounds delicious. Do you feel up to dessert? Cake?"

"Yes, cake sounds wonderful. There's a bakery next to the bistro, right?" Cammie flipped the covers back. "I'd love one of their chocolate pastries. And I think I will take a shower while you're gone."

"I'll make sure every bit of your food is safe, Cammie." Ben opened her cabin door. "If you need anything while I'm gone, just pick up the phone. It goes directly to my earpiece."

"Will do. Thanks, Ben!" Cammie waited for the door to close before she jumped out of bed. She was still wearing the infirmary gown, so she quickly changed into a pair of yoga pants and a sweater, knowing that the freezer would be super cold. She wasn't entirely sure how she'd get into the freezer without being seen, but she'd figure it out. The main thing was getting down there quickly so she could use every second of her stolen time.

She did feel slightly guilty for sending Ben on a fool's errand, but she'd give him a very generous tip when this was all said and done so, hopefully, he'd forgive her.

* * * *

It was actually ridiculously easy to get into the fridge where the freezer was located.

Cammie was a firm believer of the 'fake it 'til you make it' philosophy, a tried-and-true method of convincing everyone around you that you belonged, were capable and best of all, in charge. She'd sought out and had found a discarded clipboard on her way down to the galley, had slid a menu under the clip, grabbed a pen, then had walked right into the galley like she had business there. It had taken her a few seconds to process where the entrance to the fridge was, but as soon as she did, she beelined right for it and no one had stopped her. No one, as far as she could tell, had even glanced at her, even when she'd slipped on a, much too big, parka that had been hanging with others next to the fridge door.

Step one, get into the 'so cold her nipples had icicles' fridge — check!

Step two, figure out where in the cavernous space, a freezer would be and also where a dead body could be hidden. Luckily, the fridge lights turned on with sensors, so as she moved through the space, she wasn't heading into darkness. Of course, that meant that as she left space behind her, the maw of darkness closed in. *Very creepy!* She figured as long as she didn't look over her shoulder, she'd be fine.

The fridge had to be the size of a quarter of the ship. There were metal shelves with crates and boxes of food. There was even a forklift parked to the side. And while there were many nooks and crannies, nothing jumped out at Cammie as being an entrance to a deep freeze.

The farther she went, the colder it seemed. Her breath gusted out in great big plumbs of frosty mist and her face was numb, along with her fingers and she hadn't even gotten to the coldest part yet! The coat she'd grabbed was way too big for her, so even zipping it up left too much open at the collar and base. Cold hair filtered up and down, making her shiver, despite her sweater underneath.

She finally saw another door that looked like it could be a freezer. And, although every nerve in her body was pinging her to go the other way, she headed straight for it. The door itself was heavy, but once she got it moving, it swung easily and revealed a room full of meat—huge, hanging slabs of meat. There were also huge empty hooks that would be perfect for hanging a dead guy's body on…if she were living in some mafia crime novel. *Such morbid thoughts. Ick.* No way she was going to step foot in there. It was too ripe for murder, and she was so not the kind of girl to pull a too-stupid-to-live-move. She closed the door, for once heeding her gut, which was screaming at this point to run the other way, warm up then fetch Zane and have someone, at the very least, know what she was up to.

"Cammie, what are you doing down here?" Ben's voice came out of the darkness and startled Cammie so hard that she screamed.

"Oh my…Ben…you scared the life out of me." She gasped through her words, her heart pounding at hyper speed. "What are *you* doing down here?"

"I came to find you." Ben closed the distance between them, all sign of his usual bubbly self replaced by his frantic, hand-wringing worry. "You can't just take off like that. I need to know where you'll be. I'm supposed to keep an eye on you."

Cammie smiled, despite how frozen her cheeks were. "Oh, Ben, that's sweet, but I'm okay. I thought I'd come down and find one of those ice cream bars you told me about."

Ben frowned. "The ones that you didn't eat? They're still in your freezer in your cabin."

"They are?" Cammie gestured a 'oh duh' head slap.

Ben moved to her side then wrapped an arm around her waist. "Let's get you back into your bed where you'll be safe." He started leading her toward the exit.

"Well, actually, I need to find Zane. Do you know where he might be?" She noted how firm Ben's grip was on her side and wondered just how seriously he took his job of protecting her.

Ben stopped walking. He closed his eyes then let out a sigh.

"You just couldn't mind your own business, could you?" His voice came out like a whine. "You just had to snoop."

"Ben, I—"

"You saw, didn't you?" He tightened his grip on her. "I promised I'd keep you out of trouble, but you're so sneaky." He turned toward her with tears in his eyes. "I tried to protect you, Cammie. I tried, but you just wouldn't stop snooping, and now you have your proof and I can't let you leave here."

The horrific truth cascaded over her like someone had dumped a bucket of cold water on her head. "I-I-I didn't see anything, Ben. I swear." The truth sounded like a lie by the way her teeth chattered.

The look of pity he cut her way made any more words die in her mouth. "It's too late, Cammie," Ben croaked. "I have to take care of things now. I have to take care of you."

Ben was wearing a thick coat and gloves that fit him way better than the one Cammie had on. The cold wasn't affecting him like it was affecting her. She couldn't stop shaking, and her teeth chattered as Ben led her farther into the fridge and toward the freezer.

"I thought drugging your drink would put you out of commission long enough to get through the trip. I thought it would preoccupy Mr. Roberts as well." Ben shook his head like he was really annoyed by Cammie not staying down after he'd put her down. "But the both of you couldn't stay out of it."

It was unfathomable, like her frozen brain just would not, *could not* accept that Ben had been the one to slip Rohypnol into her drink, but he was already nodding, already confirming what she couldn't believe.

He opened the door to the freezer. Cold air blasted her in the face, freezing her eyes so she had to blink the pain away.

"Ben, please, I didn't see—"

He shoved her in the room, and she fell to her hands and knees. The cold floor burned her palms and cut through the flimsy fabric of her pants. She pushed herself up, but her fingers ached, along with her knees.

"Death by misadventure," Ben said. "I read it in a thriller once. A passenger on a cruise gets trapped in the freezer, dies of hypothermia. Sounds unbelievable but it's possible. I'll even put the ice cream bar in your hand so it looks like you just couldn't resist the captain's treats." Ben tugged the back of her coat. "Take this off. You don't need it anymore."

"Ben..." Cammie closed her eyes. A tear slipped from her eye then froze on her cheek. "You don't have to do this." She unzipped her coat anyway.

"I wish I didn't, Cammie. I really do." He pulled her jacket from her arms and the cold enveloped her like a frosty blanket. "I've heard dying this way isn't that bad."

Cammie glared over her shoulder at him.

"Don't worry, Cammie." He tossed her coat to the floor, then crouched down to sit on it. A front row seat to her death. At least he had the courtesy to look appalled. "I'll stay with you, so you won't die alone."

Chapter Twenty

Zane hadn't passed out, but with the way his head had been throbbing over the last few hours, he wished he had.

Sherri had an event, and Elm had an interview with Chief Ross, so they'd decided to leave Zane's murder until later.

Lucky me.

Elm had given him another whack to the head before tying his arms behind his back with a belt and gagging him with a pillowcase. Zane had been in too much pain to do anything about it for longer than he cared to admit.

While his brain was foggy from what he was sure was another concussion he couldn't afford to endure, he knew time was ticking and he had to get out of this situation before they came back. He tested the belt only to find it was secured with expertise. No way he'd be able to wiggle his way out of it, even if he could dislocate one of his joints — which he couldn't.

He had to get to Cammie and make sure she was safe. He had to warn the captain. But first, he had to save himself.

Moving too quickly would probably make him vomit, which would be a very bad thing with the pillowcase wedged in his mouth so that was the first thing that had to go. He focused on cracking his jaw as wide as he could, then slowly, painstakingly, eased the wad of cloth away from this throat with his tongue. It took some time and made his headache bloom all over again, but eventually the last of the pillowcase fell from this mouth. He lay on his side, panting, as lightning struck across his brain over and over.

The beating he'd taken while he'd been in the service, the one that had put him in a coma, had resulted in a lifetime ban of anything that could jar his brain in even the slightest way—no trampolines, no jogging, no beat downs from an old guy. He knew Elm had done some significant damage and that he needed medical attention. The way his head was screaming, he knew that it was only a matter of time before he'd black out, and if he blacked out, he was a dead man. Lying around on the floor wasn't going to get him what he needed. Neither was shouting, though, because Zane knew just as well as Elm did that no one would hear him on a deserted deck.

But someone could *see* him.

Zane took a few solid breaths, testing the pain threshold of his diaphragm from when Elm had nailed him there, but the damage was minimal and the pain manageable.

He curled his knees to his chest, moving like a snail so he didn't jar his head any more than he had to. Then he pushed his bound hands up to act as a leverage as he eased himself to his knees.

Dizziness sent black streaks over his vision, and he rested his forehead to the floor, inhaling all manner of dust and dirt to keep himself conscious.

He gave himself a few minutes, enough time to clear the cobwebs so he could try again. He used his core muscles to lift his upper body, moving gingerly so he didn't see stars. He got to his knees, rested for a few breaths, then used the door to hold him steady as he pushed himself to his feet. The world tilted and his legs wobbled, but he knew that if he didn't get himself out of this cabin, he was a dead man. He might be a dead man anyway, but he at least had to try.

Zane slid himself to the door handle then used his bound hands to push down. It wasn't a problem since his height worked to his advantage. What wasn't working was hooking the handle at the same time so he could walk it open. Not only were his hands slipping off the handle but his legs also refused to cooperate. His vision swished from light to dark to light again, and he knew he was close to hitting the floor, because the pain in his head had escalated to A-bomb status. By the buzzing in his ears, he was seconds away from passing out.

He wasn't going to let Elm or Sherri get away with their crimes, even if he had to sacrifice himself to shine a spotlight on them.

He closed his eyes then heaved the door with as much brute strength as he could gather. It only opened wide enough for his massive body to slither out, but that was all he needed. He wedged himself through the opening, then let himself fall, landing with a thud that likely shook the ceiling on the next deck.

Chapter Twenty-One

Cammie's lungs filled with icicles, her muscles spasmed like frost had slipped inside them and her teeth chattered so bad that she was sure her tongue wasn't safe if she said a word.

Luckily, she didn't have to.

"I've heard it's quite painless to die of hypothermia once the cold really sets in." Ben crossed his legs like this was a *Romper Room* sing-along circle. "Your organs shut down then you just fall asleep."

He had the nerve to shiver, like he was actually feeling the cold with his layers on, like she was without protection at all.

"Can I hold your hand?" Ben shifted forward.

Cammie nodded. It would save her from having to move to him.

He scooted closer, shifting until he could clasp her hand in his. Even with his gloves on, his gesture offered her no warmth.

She curled her near-frozen fingers around his then yanked him forward as she spun on her ass, ignoring the way the cold ripped through her clothes to bite at her skin. She wrapped her legs around Ben's waist.

He fell forward, shock flashing across his face.

She didn't give him time to register anything beyond that.

She hooked her ankles behind his back, locking him in as she knocked his flailing arm away then gripped the furry collar of his coat and hauled him into her. A puff of frozen mist escaped from his parted lips just before Cammie twisted her hips then flipped him under her. She straddled him in one fluid move, adrenaline warming her up, melting the ice that had invaded her body. Despite his initial shock, Ben tried to reach up to hold her back, but she forced his arm out of the way as she used her knee to hold his head down. Something crunched. It could have been his nose, but she didn't care. Then she shifted back and to the side, taking his hand with her, yanking it into an arm bar that made the bone groan in her grip.

"Don't move or I'll break it." Her breath came out in a whoosh.

"You can't!" Ben whined. "Please, don't!"

"I swear to you, Ben, that I can and I will." She tugged again, a fraction of a movement away from snapping his bone.

"It hurts! Please stop!" The tears streaming down his cheeks gave off heat before they frozen to his skin. Blood pooled around his nose and mouth and quickly turned to frozen mush. "Please don't, Cammie. I'll tell you everything. I promise. Please!"

"What the fuck is going on here?" Cammie knew she had minutes before the cold seeped past the adrenaline rush and incapacitated her again.

"I had to put Frankie somewhere." Ben's teeth chattered, from fear or cold, Cammie didn't know.

Even though she knew she wasn't delusional, there was a sense of validation to get confirmation that she had indeed found a dead man on her floor. "I put him in your room because I saw you leave the sunset mixer with Zane and figured I had time. I needed to wait for the shift change so I could bring him here."

"Why did you kill him? Wasn't he your friend?" Or at least his roommate? Was it possible that Ben wanted to be part of the event crew so badly that he'd murdered for it? Her gut rejected that idea though. Ben might be stupid, but he hadn't come across as petty.

"I didn't! I swear!" Ben cried. "Ms-s-s. B-B-Bolt did. S-she poisoned him!"

"Sherri?" Cammie was surprised enough to release her death grip somewhat and give Ben's arm a rest.

"Yes, Sherri!" Ben gasped. "She did it because Frankie was stealing too much money and her dad told her to deal with him. She didn't want to kill him—I know she didn't—but you don't say no to a man like Elm Stone—"

"Wait a minute." Cammie let Ben's arm go completely then straddled him again, pushing her weight down so his hips were pinned. "Elm Stone, Bill Haversmith's buddy, is Sherri's father?"

"Yes! That's what I'm saying." Ben tried to touch his nose now that his hands were free, but he was whimpering and shaking too much to actually do it. "He's been cleaning money on the cruises, and Frankie was involved. Sherri said he was skimming off the top and took way too much, so her dad wanted him gone. I didn't know!" Ben raised his hands as if to ward off a blow. "Sherri asked me to help her, and of course, stupid me, I jumped at the chance. When I went to her cabin, Frankie was already dead. Elm told me to take care of the body."

"Jesus Christ, Ben, why didn't you tell anyone?" Cammie shook her head. "You could have gotten help."

"I'm a horrible person." Ben broke down, his body shaking as he sobbed. "Sherri told me I could take over Frankie's job. She said she's made sure I was rewarded. She's so incredible, and I thought… I thought she really cared about my future."

He worshipped Sherri enough to be an accomplice to murder?

"And me? Did Elm tell you to kill me too?" Cammie leaned forward, bracing her forearm on Ben's chest, putting pressure on his lungs.

"He was so mad that the Rohypnol didn't work." Ben tried to push her arm away, but she wasn't going anywhere. Let him get a taste of being defenseless and at someone else's mercy. "I gave it to him when you and Mr. Haversmith were off looking at something in the Burlesque Bar and told him to put the whole vial in, but he didn't have time."

Elm had been sitting across the table from her. He could have easily slipped something into her drink before she got back from her mini-excursion with Bill.

"And he wants me dead?" Cammie eased her hold against Ben's chest.

"He said there was no other way." Ben hiccupped through his tears. "He said he was going to take care of Mr. Roberts himself."

"Where is he now?" Cammie jumped up. "Where is Elm *now*?" If Zane were in trouble, she had to help him.

"I don't know!" Ben cried. "The last time I saw him he was on his way to meet with Chief Ross."

"Is the chief in on this too?" Cammie was already at the freezer door.

"No! He's interviewing everyone who was around you in the Burlesque Room, trying to figure out who drugged you." Ben shifted so he was sitting up. "I'm sorry, Cammie. I'm so sorry! I don't think Elm has killed Mr. Roberts yet."

Yet.

A word that didn't inspire confidence. "How do you know?"

"When I came back to your room with food and realized you were missing, I panicked and called Sherri. She's working an event all afternoon and told me to find Elm." Ben sucked in a few breaths. "He didn't let me explain what had happened. He just said that he needed me to babysit Zane, but he couldn't tell me where Mr. Roberts was because security had found him right then and asked had him to come for his interview."

Fuck!

She needed to find Zane, and she needed help to do it. The last time she'd tried to get the Security Chief to believe her story, she didn't have proof. Cammie stormed to Ben and he cried out, cowering as she approached. She took his hand and twisted it behind his back, using pain as incentive to get Ben up.

"Ouch! Please don't break my arm!" Ben might have had several feet on Cammie but size really didn't matter when the right pressure was applied. "Where are we going?"

She marched him to the door.

"We're going to solve a murder and save the hero and, this time, everyone's going to believe me."

Chapter Twenty-Two

"You missed all the fun." Cammie's voice wafted into Zane's ears like an ocean breeze.

He slit his eyes open enough to see her sitting next to him. He was no longer on a musty floor, and his head pain had subsided from the beat of a full marching band to a low-key acoustic version. "What happened?"

"We stopped the bad guys." Cammie squeezed his hand. "We closed your case."

"We?" As far as Zane could remember, he'd done nothing more than get himself beaten up, so if that's what had cracked the case, he should thank Elm. "I'm pretty sure I face-planted on the floor and didn't accomplish shit."

"Your swan dive into the hallway outside of Sherri's cabin alerted security to a problem," Cammie said. "They sent medics, and Chief Ross himself sought Sherri out to question why a semi-conscious man had stumbled from her cabin."

"I bet she couldn't explain that." Given how high-strung Sherri seemed to be in general, Zane guessed she didn't really have a poker face when it came down to it.

"Nope, she cracked immediately, spewing a confession before they could even clear her from the event she was managing. She made quite the scene, apparently. Drama galore. She implicated Elm and Ben—"

"Ben, your steward?" He tried to push himself up but was still too dizzy to do much more than nod his head.

"Here... Let me help." Cammie adjusted his bed so he wasn't lying flat on his back. She slid another pillow behind his head to prop him up more. "And yes, Ben was the one who put Frankie's body in my room, then removed it to store in the ship's freezer."

"Wow, he wasn't even on my radar." And really, Elm hadn't been either, which made Zane wonder if he was really cut out for this kind of investigative work after all. He should probably stick to debt collection and leave the detective work to someone without a head injury.

"Nope, I'd never have believed Ben was involved. He'd put on a good innocent act, Oscar-worthy for sure, but he confessed, too." She was back to holding his hand, and he had to admit, he liked the comfort of having someone with him when he was injured.

All the time he'd spent in hospital after his coma, he'd had no visitors. No one besides the nurses and his doctor seemed to give a shit about him at all. It was his first real taste of loneliness, something he'd never left behind him but something that seemed safer than letting another person into his dark world of self-pity and trauma responses.

"And Elm? Tell me security got him before he could jump overboard." He laughed but regretted it immediately when fireworks exploded across the front of his brain. He squeezed his eyes shut and prayed he wouldn't barf all over himself in front of Cammie.

"Oh, Zane, you can't do that. No sudden movements." Cammie put something in his hand. "Press the button for pain meds."

He pressed the button three times, hoping that it meant triple the dose of whatever was in the IV. The effect was almost instantaneous. Relief came in ebbing waves, soothing over the fire of his headache but also nudging him toward the darkness where there was no Cammie and no comfort.

He fought to keep his eyes open but only managed to crack them. "Thank you," he croaked.

Cammie didn't seem to need an explanation. She caressed his hand and smiled. "Get some sleep, Zane."

"I don't want... I want to..." His words jumbled in his mouth.

"I'll be here when you wake up." Her words floated through his awareness.

"I couldn't...do this...without you." Even though he had no idea how he closed the case at all. There were still too many holes to fill. Missing pieces that were hovering somewhere just out of his reach. "I'm sorry...your vacation...ruined." His mouth was full of cotton balls.

"Are you kidding? This was the best vacation I've had in like...forever! Mystery, intrigue, sex and kink all rolled up in almost five days." She winked just before his eyes slid closed. "I wouldn't have it any other way." He felt her lips on his cheek. "Okay, I could probably do without the dead body, frostbite and you suffering from a concussion."

Frostbite? His brain grew fuzzier by the second, rolling fog seeped into his thoughts and made it harder to focus on her words. He wanted to ask her to explain but instead he said, "I like you." And hoped that she understood that this wasn't just a fling to him anymore.

* * * *

"How are the patients doing?" Captain Evans swept into the infirmary with a cheery wave at the nurse.

Cammie bristled. While he'd taken action when confronted with the proof that Cammie wasn't out of her mind, he still hadn't apologized for not believing her in the first place.

"Both are stable, Captain," the nurse drawled from her desk.

"Good to hear!" He walked to Zane's bed, actively avoiding Cammie's death glare. "We've arranged for paramedics to be on site when we dock, so Mr. Roberts will not experience a huge disruption in care."

Cammie clenched the hand on her lap, ignoring the pain from the frostbite to her fingers. She'd been treated and the damage wasn't too severe, according to the nurse, but she'd need some follow-up care at the hospital as well.

"And you, Miss Sheppard? How are your fingers?" He finally looked over at her then recoiled from the expression on her face.

"This could have all been prevented had you believed me in the first place." Cammie gave him a sugary smile full of poison. "None of this would have happened if you had investigated instead of leaving it to Zane and me."

"Yes, well, uh..." he sputtered. "It seemed unplausible that...uh..."

"Yet there was a body in the freezer, correct?" She already knew the answer because Chief Ross had stopped in at the infirmary to check on things and had updated her just before Zane had woken up.

"Yes, unfortunately, we did find the body of a deceased male." Captain Evans cleared his throat. "So, it appears that you did, in fact, find a dead body in your cabin."

"Hmm." Cammie noted the captain's lack of apology. "Tell me something…" She made sure he was looking at her. "Do you think, my boss, Sabine Cowan, will keep you on as captain after I tell her how gloriously you fucked this up?"

His face bloomed red as he opened his mouth, then closed it, gaping like a fish desperate for air.

"After I told her about Cal's failing fetish cruise business, she got on the phone with the bank right away. She and Cal go way back, and she's been looking at expanding Cowan Enterprises into the travel industry for a while now. All it took was my endorsement—you know, because she values my opinion so much." Cammie reveled in the captain's obvious discomfort. "She's negotiating with your brother as we speak. He seems eager to unload the ships now that he knows just how bad things have gotten."

"I do apologize, Miss Sheppard," Captain Evans said, the smug smile finally wiped from his face. "I, uh, was focused on the missing money and saving the company."

Cammie nodded but didn't give him the benefit of a response. Let him wonder what she would say to Sabine. She turned back to Zane.

The captain stood there for an awkward few minutes, clearly unsure how to proceed.

She wanted him gone and knew she'd have to be the one to dismiss him now that she'd cut his balls off. "You better make sure there are no hitches in my boyfriend's care, Captain, or Sabine will hear about it from me." She didn't bother looking up at him to deliver her warning, partly because she was sick of the sight of him but partly because the word 'boyfriend' had slipped out and her brain was recalibrating.

"Of course, Miss Sheppard, I'll make another call right now to ensure that Mr. Roberts gets the best care there is." He didn't wait for her to acknowledge that she'd heard him, he practically speed walked out of the door with a curt goodbye to the nurse.

Cammie smiled to herself as she brushed her fingers, the undamaged ones, along Zane's cheek and accepted the fact that somewhere along the way, her heart and her head had decided he was the one for her. It was unexpected and unplanned, but it suited Cammie perfectly.

Epilogue

Six months later

As a card-carrying workaholic, Cammie wouldn't have guessed that she'd be on vacation twice in one year.

"Don't forget, Cammie. You're supposed to relax this time," Sabine's disembodied voice reminded her. "You're quality control."

"Oh, I'm definitely going to relax." Cammie adjusted the straps of her outfit. "It's all fun and games from this point on."

"Good." Sabine was aboard one of the other ships for the maiden voyage of the Kitty Cat Cruise Line. There were five ships in total, all themed differently. "I'm going to indulge, too."

"There's only one way to make sure our guests are having a great time and that's to experience it ourselves." Cammie slipped her heels on. "I'll touch base with you tomorrow."

"Sounds like a plan." Sabine hung up, leaving Cammie to check the mirror one last time.

She could have chosen to supervise the murder mystery cruise, but both she and Zane felt like they'd kinda had enough of that type of intrigue for a while. There was the escape room and bondage cruise, but Adam and Missy had opted for that one. Sabine was aboard the Wild West cruise with Trent, and Vivian and her boys were checking out the ghostly encounters cruise, which had various port stops to tour haunted places.

Cammie had selected the fun and games cruise because it had felt right that Zane and she celebrate six months of being together with some play.

Six months. She'd never had a relationship last as long, but now that she did, she was ready to do the dirty in role-play form.

Zane was waiting for her in their designated room, so she slipped out of their suite then headed down to one of three role-play decks.

After Sabine had bought out Cal's fetish cruise line, she'd spent a buttload to revamp the ships, transforming them from just okay to fucking fabulous. She'd gutted cabins, repurposing them for private playrooms that had limited the number of guests who could get on board—and that had driven the price up to purchase a coveted spot on one of the ships. There was a waitlist in the hundreds that was growing by the day, and after the maiden voyages, which included some strategically placed influencers, those lists would explode.

"Hey, Cammie!" Elena, one of the Cats, came sauntering toward her, all decked out in latex that looked painted on and hugged her generous curves so seductively that Cammie wondered if she could pull that kind of thing off. "Love that outfit."

"Thanks, love yours, too, a lot." Cammie walked with Elena into the elevator. "How are things going in your room?" Sabine had invested hundreds of thousands of dollars to create variously themed areas for group play. Elena managed the tag game, which was set up to look like a city but was rigged to allow all manner of climbing and jumping, running and hiding—the perfect set-up for folks who liked to chase or be chased.

"Amazing, of course." Elena preened. "We're just getting a new game started if you want to check it out."

"Maybe later." Cammie nodded to deck button she'd pressed. "I've got plans this afternoon."

"Ohh-h, yes, you do." Elena winked. "Have fun!"

"Thanks, lady. I'll catch you later." The doors opened and Cammie walked out. Now that she was steps away from seeing Zane all decked out in his costume, butterflies ruffled her stomach, and she couldn't keep the grin off her face.

They'd been able to maintain a long-distance relationship while he'd settled things up after the Dark Matter cruise. He'd needed time to recover from his head injury and sell his place in Daytona. He'd insisted that he'd never really loved the sun and sand and had been meaning to spend more long-term time in New York, a place he'd only visited here and there before. But she'd suspected that he was as into her as she was into him, and he'd moved to her hometown three months before. They'd been enjoying each other ever since. He'd done a few freelance jobs for Sabine as well as continuing his own PI work—no murder investigations, just hunting down merchandise like missing boats and expensive cars that had loan defaults.

Being on this cruise together would be the first time they'd had more than a handful of hours to enjoy one another's company without work getting in the way.

She stopped outside Role-Play Room number four and took a deep breath — well, as big as her outfit would allow — then let it out slowly. She straightened her corset, making sure her cleavage still popped but that her nipples didn't quite poke out yet. This was a big step for her. Role play was always reserved for special relationships, committed relationships, because it demanded that Cammie step way out of her comfort zone.

Zane was on the other side of the door, waiting. She lifted her hand, turned the knob, then stepped into another world.

"Don't move." Zane's rough voice made her toes curl. "Where's your ID?"

"I told you who I am. Why do you need proof?" Cammie's arms were behind her back, both wrists in the strong vise grip of Zane's one hand.

He yanked her back so her spine arched. "Don't be sassy." He growled against her ear, sending shivers along her skin. "Give me your ID."

"It's between my boobs," she bit back. "There's no way you're squeezing it outta my corset."

"Don't be so sure about that." Zane laughed in a dark and dangerous way. He slipped his hand over her hip, up her corset to the tie that held it all together. "One tug and I get what I want."

"You won't get away with this." Cammie tried to shake herself free but there was no getting out of his hold on her wrists.

"It's you who won't get away." He tugged the ties binding her corset closed and unraveled the top portion. Her tits pushed against the stiff fabric, forcing her nipples to peek over the top. "You owe me money. Never paid me for my investigation."

"I don't know what you're talking about. I've paid everything I owe." Cammie squirmed as Zane slid his thick fingers into her corset to pull her ID out.

He brushed the back of his hand against one beaded nipple before holding her ID up for both of them to read.

"Looks like I got the right person after all. You should have known a disguise wouldn't work, Miss Sheppard." With lightning-fast reflexes, Zane whipped out handcuffs then secured them over her wrists before she could blink. "You're coming with me to lock-up. And don't think whining to the judge about being broke will get you anywhere. We had a deal. You didn't pay."

"No, please no! I'll do anything. Please!" She tried to turn but Zane had a firm grip on her binding, holding her in place. "I can't go to jail! I'll die in there."

Zane leaned closer. "No, but you'll probably wish you had." He slipped his hand to her exposed nipples, brushing across both with his open palm. "But I suppose I'm willing to negotiate something."

He tugged the opening of her corset, loosening it even more so both tits spilled out.

"But it's gonna cost you." He cupped both breasts as he kissed along the side of her neck. "I'm not a cheap man to buy, and you already owe me, sooo…"

Her legs wobbled. Her pussy throbbed. Her nipples perked up even more, aching as he rolled them roughly between his thumb and fingers.

He nipped her earlobe and she melted.

"On your knees." He pushed her down so that she hit the floor hard then circled her, appraising her submission like she was a misbehaving animal. "What will you pay me to let you go?" He circled again. "You have no money, obviously." He paused in front of her, his fingers on the zipper of his slacks. "Will you take my cock down your throat?"

Cammie nodded. "All the way down."

Zane raised an eyebrow. "Oh really?" He unzipped. "I'm not sure you're prepared for my cock."

Cammie licked her lips as she looked up at him through her eyelashes. "I've got a big mouth."

Zane's lips quirked but he didn't laugh. "We'll see about that." He opened his pants, and his cock sprang out, the tip glistening with pre-cum.

Cammie shifted forward, shuffling on her knees to get closer. She licked the dab of cum from Zane's slit, savoring the salty tang before rubbing her tongue along his shaft then over his balls.

"Good girl." He moaned as he slipped his fingers into her hair.

She made her way back up his shaft, licking and flicking along this crown until she was right back where she started. His cock was huge and thick, but she was sure she could take him all the way down—after all, she had before. He nudged his cock against her lips and tugged at her hair, letting her know she was wasting his time. She opened her mouth until her jaw popped then swallowed him whole. When the tip of his dick hit the back of her throat, she adjusted, tilted back a little, then welcomed him all the way.

She hummed and he groaned, his fingers digging into her scalp to hold her in place as he rocked himself back and forth, fucking her mouth and her throat as her tits swayed and her nipples brushed against the open zipper of his pants.

She thought he might spew just from her blow job, but he pulled back before his thrusts became too urgent.

"Get up," he ordered once he'd slipped his cock from her lips.

She scrambled to do as he'd said, saliva and pre-cum dripping down her chin as she struggled to get up quickly.

"Turn around." He grabbed her wrists once she had her back to him then unlocked one handcuff. "Put your arms in front of you."

She did as she was told and he quickly re-cuffed her, then hoisted her arms up as he moved her backward, his face inches from hers, his eyes blasting with heat. Her ass hit the wall, followed by her shoulders. Zane hooked the cuffs above her head so she had to stretch, practically on her tiptoes.

"You're at *my* mercy now." He grinned. "I'm going to make you earn your freedom."

He pulled the rest of the binding of her corset so it slipped from her body then fell to the floor with a thud. The cool air caressed her nipples, making them bud. She wanted Zane's mouth to warm her up, but instead he moved out of her line of vision.

She heard the snap of leather pulling taut then felt the bite of the whip against her tits. She arched away from another strike but with nowhere to go, she really was at his mercy. The whip hit again, stinging along the top of her breasts, licking at her nipples so that they exploded with fire.

He moved in front of her, whip in hand and expression all business. "You're going to wish you'd paid up on time before I'm done with you."

He sank to his knees then lifted her skirt with the tip of the whip handle. She wasn't wearing panties, of course, so she felt his hot breath against her pussy immediately.

"I know just how to torture a lady like you," he said. "Let's see how many times you can come in one night, shall we?"

He rubbed the whip handle along her pussy lips, poking at her clit roughly. She wiggled and squirmed, but he gripped her hip with one hand then shoved his face between her legs, rubbing his nose against her slit, then his tongue, teasing her with soft, probing caresses. She moaned when he latched onto her sensitive nub, her body contorting against the wall as he sucked her hard with his mouth and used the whip handle to fuck her pussy.

Her climax was thunder and lightning, sparks flying, uncontrollable and unstoppable. Her pussy spasmed and clenched around the whip as Zane relentlessly licked and flicked her clit. He wrung her out, then kept going, ignoring her writhing, knocking her foot away from his shoulder when she tried to shove him back and pushed her body to the brink of another explosion so close on the heels of the last one.

This time her orgasm was a slow burning fire, raging just beneath the surface, steadily growing fiercer, as her nerves, wrung out and sensitive from the last one, pinged and twinged, making her moan long and low. He pulled his mouth away then used his thumb to press hard on her clit, rubbing her roughly, until she couldn't do anything but let the climax consume her, racking her body with shuddering waves.

Her body was coated in sweat, her skin so on edge that even the cool air was enough to tease her.

Zane stood, whip in hand, his cock hard and jutting from his pants. He gripped her hips then spun her, twisting her arms over her head to pull on the handcuffs so they bit into her wrists.

He cupped her tits then pinched her nipples. She opened her mouth to cry out but the whip searing her ass cheeks made her swallow down any noise.

He didn't hold back, whacking her relentlessly until her skin was on fire.

She rocked her hips, moving into the next strike, welcoming it, but instead of feeling another slap of leather, Zane thrust his cock into her deeply, making her gasp. He reached around to finger her clit. She couldn't take it. Every nerving ending in her body detonated like tiny A-bombs, sending cascading waves through her body until her brain turned to mush and her legs wobbled.

Zane drilled her pussy, punishing her with his cock, rubbing his finger roughly against her clit, spiking her climax, revving her up and up. She couldn't take it! It was too much!

He pulled out and she gasped again as he spun her around, coaxing her legs around his waist. His eyes were hooded, his face coated in sweat. He pinioned her to the wall, sheathing himself with one thrust. He lowered his mouth to her nipple, sucking half her tit into his mouth as he pumped her pussy. She flexed her back, arching against him, trying to get closer, even though they were fused. He cupped her tits, covering her aching nubs, then kissed her. His lips on hers were fire and ice, redemption and punishment, all at the same time.

He sucked on her tongue, squeezed her tits and fucked her pussy. Her body pulsed, her climax started, ringing from her core outward to every nerve ending. Zane bellowed as his cock throbbed inside her, spewing his load in hot jets, jolting her orgasm to match his.

She shook and screamed and lost her mind in the best possible way.

As they slowly came down from their high, Zane floated his gaze up to meet hers. He had a lazy grin on his face, an expression of a satisfied man.

"Paid in full," he growled.

Cammie giggled, her body a loose noodle. "Oh, I don't know about that." She rolled her hips.

He raised an eyebrow.

She winked.

Then they both laughed their asses off and Cammie, once again, felt like she'd hit the jackpot, finding the perfect guy to have fun with.

Want to see more from this author?
Here's a taster for you to enjoy!

Must Love Cats
Angela Addams

Excerpt

Lucki

Cat Keeper of Weeping Falls. It sounds like a joke, right? Cat Keeper… What the hell kind of job is that?

"The best job in the mothereff" —*burp*— "ing world!" Lucki Collins raised her almost empty pint of beer and cheered the crowd of rowdy townspeople who were seated all around her. The burn of too much booze heated her cheeks, and the ache from so much laughing had her cradling her side. She was being treated like a queen and didn't care if she was making an ass of herself.

"Cheers to our new Cat Keeper. May your time here be ever filled with joy." Mr. Rose an elderly man with a bright red nose and long white whiskers, raised his glass, which was filled with…milk. It was the only thing he'd been drinking all night.

Lucki figured it had to be mixed with bourbon or something. The man was way too cheerful to be sober. *They're all way too cheerful.* The entire town of Weeping Falls, a population of a hundred at most, had welcomed her with open arms the second she'd cleared the town line — and hadn't stopped welcoming her.

"To our blessed Cat Keeper!" Everyone cheered, raising their glasses, thumping on the tables, laughing, singing.

They were in the tavern, a throwback to the old West, complete with its swinging doors and long curved bar, plank wood floors that were scuffed and dented and an old-time piano that one of the residents had been playing since Lucki had gotten there. Everyone was dressed in the fashion of the time too — from the cowboy hats to the heel spurs, corsets and billowing skirts. Lucki truly felt like she'd stepped into the olden days — and she loved it.

Weeping Falls had been an actual mining town back in the day. Now it was barely hanging on as a ghost town tourist attraction — the Wild West in Alaska. There wasn't much in the way of bookings, from what she'd gathered. The only visitor was her, and she was soon to be a resident too. She'd be Lady Clover's Cat Keeper, responsible for tending to a massive cat colony who'd been bequeathed a mansion and a trust fund and who called Weeping Falls home.

When she'd been offered the job, she'd thought she'd heard wrong.

"Cat keeper? What kind of job is that?"

Scout, the man who'd found her, had answered her simply and honestly. *"We can't afford a trained vet to come. You have almost all the requirements and a lot of experience working with animals. You'll do."*

Lucki had been working at shelters her whole life. Always a tender heart around those injured or in need of love, she'd solely manned a cat sanctuary in her hometown until a fire had taken out the entire colony the past summer. It had nearly destroyed her heart to lose all those precious lives.

Scout had come knocking on her door one morning, claiming he'd heard about her compassion toward the felines and had wanted to offer her a new job as Cat Keeper for Lady Clover's Cat House in Weeping Falls, Alaska.

It had seemed like a good idea at the time—a windfall, actually. Everyone knew she was destined to be a crazy cat lady anyway, and now she was going to be paid to fulfill that dream. It sounded pretty freakin' perfect to her.

Besides, she had another reason to leave home—a big, six-foot-two, built-like-a-brick-house reason whom she wanted no reminder of ever again. He'd be in jail for another year at least, and by the time he got out, he'd find no trace of her. That gave her some measure of peace.

Her heart had been crushed, battered and beaten enough over the last ten years. She needed this escape, and Scout's offer had come at the perfect moment. Time would heal all wounds—or so she'd heard—but cuddling with a bunch of cats would make that time sweeter.

And there hadn't been a moment of regret—not one. She'd spent more than a day on the road with only a brief stop to rest, travelling all the way from her hometown in northern British Columbia.

It was a long way to come for a bunch of cats.

Best decision ever!

She downed what was left of her beer then snorted in the most unladylike way when another full pint slid in front of her.

"Oh boy, no way!" She laughed. "You people are going to get me totally wasted."

"Aww, lass, no harm," Andy Crawlie drawled. "We're just happy yer finally here. We've been waitin' on ya fer a vera long time."

That had been what it had been like the entire night. They'd fed her delicious food until she was stuffed, then they'd started pouring the beer, keeping her glass full while they sang and laughed and told stories. There were enough people in the tavern that she lost track of all the names and keeping everyone straight. But she had plenty of time to learn them.

Lucki giggled but pushed the glass away. "Thank you for all your generosity, everyone." She had to raise her voice to be heard over the music playing. "I think I should head back to Lady Clover's, though. It's late... Wait! How late is it?" Her phone had stopped working at some point during the night. She imagined that cell service was spotty at best around here anyway. She made a mental note to ask someone about it in the morning when her thoughts were clearer.

"Oh, it's hardly after midnight, dear," Sandy Evernight said as she picked up Lucki's beer and took a sip for herself. "But if you must go, we'll send you with an escort, to make sure you get back to the house in one piece."

"An escort?" Lucki pushed her chair back. The wood feet thudded across the floor, giving Lucki a bit of a fight to stand.

"It's always a good idea around here." Sandy shrugged, her cheeks bright. She had a glint in her eyes that made Lucki question if there was a punchline coming. "'Cause of the wild animals and such."

"Wild animals?" Lucki frowned, her good mood taken down a notch. *Not a joke, then. Right, because you're in the middle of freakin' Alaska! Spring is coming. Of course there are animals roaming around.*

"Och, Sandy, quit scaring the girl. You want her to pick up and leave before she's even settled in?" Mr. Rose said. "Rueben's out there watchin' for her. He'll make sure she gets home safe."

"Oh, Reuben's around?" Sandy winked, aiming another sly smile at Lucki. "Didn't know. Hadn't seen him."

"Don't be daft, woman." Andy *tsk*ed.

"You'll be fine, Lucki," Mr. Rose said with a reassuring pat on her arm. "Just be sure to put your coat on. The nights are still bitter cold around here."

Someone handed Lucki her giant parka as she stood on wobbly legs, the beers rushing through her system worse than she'd first thought. "Thanks." She slipped herself inside the warm down coat and instantly shivered as the heat embraced her. It would soon be too hot to be wearing inside the tavern. That was for sure. "I'll see you all in the morning."

Everyone mumbled something at her in response, but as she moved toward the door, she realized they just as soon returned to their drinking and joking, seeming to forget all about her. Looking over her shoulder at the group, she smiled once again. *Such a fun bunch of folks.* Unusual, sure, but also warm and embracing. Their unquestioning friendliness was like a comfort blanket around her heart. And that was something she really, really needed.

She pushed through the doors and blinked against the cold bite of the air. Icy wind shot up her nose and stung her brain. Sandy had said it was spring and she wasn't wrong, calendar wise, but the weather up here was not any kind of spring that Lucki had ever experienced. Even in Canada, where the winters could get brutal, May usually came with milder temperatures, even at night.

But today was only May first, she reminded herself. *Beltane.* The familiar stir of longing rattled through her. In years past, Beltane was always a night she'd enjoyed with others. *With him.* Marking the coming of spring, Beltane was a celebration of new growth and fertility, and usually involved a night of ritual, song and dance, bonfires and, in her adult life, a lot of sexual exploration. This was the first time in many years that she would be alone.

But the past is the past, and it's better to be alone and happy than with someone and miserable.

"Blessed be," she said with a sigh.

She let her eyes adjust to the night then looked up at the impossibly bright stars overhead. She'd never seen so many in her life. She scanned the sky, hoping to see the Northern Lights, which she'd read about when she had been trying to research what to expect in Alaska, but the only light was from the stars and the moon, which was near full. *Beautiful.* She took in a deep breath, ignoring the burn of the cold air as it ripped up her nose again, freezing her nostrils. *Refreshing, sure, but also painful.* She chuckled to herself then took a few steps off the porch.

The gritty earth crunched under her feet. It was a strangely comforting sound that broke up the silence of the night and gave Lucki something to focus on other than the shadowed buildings.

The town consisted of a main strip with all the old ghost-town amenities—a barbershop with its candy-cane stripe, a hotel down the road, grocery store, shoemaker, blacksmith and even a church. There was a carriage without its horses and bundles of hay off to the side. It was so old-world and yet not. There were modern amenities as well—like the streetlamps, which were a little too far apart for Lucki's liking, and a few cars parked here and there.

She flipped up her hood, suddenly feeling the cold worse as it whipped down the back of her neck, making her shiver right to her bones. Lady Clover's Cat House was at the other end of the strip. The lights of the mansion shone from almost every window, a guiding beacon, so it would be impossible to not find her way there.

My new home. Hard to really fathom. It was three stories of old-world charm. Painted yellow like the sun, it had stained-glass multicolored windows with white shutters to frame them and a wraparound porch that could fit a hundred people with no problem. There was even a swinging chair there for her to lounge on in the warmer months, and she so looked forward to reading a few books out there with some cats on her lap. It was a house she could only dream of living in one day, and here she was walking down a dirt road, on her way to spending her first night in a castle of cats. *Bliss.*

Although this particular bliss included a pretty frosty walk. The cold bit at her cheeks and stung her eyes, so she walked faster. The noise from the partiers dimmed behind her. The silence of Alaska greeted her with each step she took toward her new home. She could fall in love with a place like this. It was so peaceful. So simple. She didn't miss the buzzing white noise that she'd grown accustomed to back home or the constant urgency to check her phone for messages. She was unplugged. Calm. At peace.

"Meow."

Lucki stopped in her tracks. *Ohhhhhhh, one of the cats?* She hadn't met any of them yet, but she was eager to.

"Kitty?"

"Meeeeeow."

She shifted her hood so she could look all around. "Here, kitty. Come here, kitty. Let me see you!" She felt no shame in her excitement over meeting the cats. She looked forward to bonding with each of them. She'd been warned it was quite a large colony, a hundred at least. "Here, kitty!"

"Meow!"

She felt a nudge against her boot and shifted her hood to look down. The coat was so bulky that she could hardly see her own feet.

"Mr. Whiskers?" she said, as she swooped down to pick up her own cat. "What are you doing out here all alone, baby?" The only cat to have survived the fire was one of her favorites, a mangy brown tabby she called Mr. Whiskers. She'd brought him with her to Alaska but had left him safe and sound in the house — or so she'd thought. "How'd you get out here?"

"Muuuuurrrrow!" He purred like an engine and nuzzled into her arms as she stroked him.

"Well, you silly boy, let's get you back inside where it's warm."

She walked, the *crunch* of her feet on the gravelly dirt road a distraction again. She pulled her attention from the ground and scanned the buildings around her.

"It's awfully dark." In between the streetlights was pitch black, and unusual shadows had collected in those places, keeping just out of reach from the lights. In each of those in-between spaces were alleys that were so opaque that they were impenetrable without a flashlight.

Creepy. The sobering reality of being completely alone in the middle of a town where she didn't really know anyone slithered down her spine. If she called out, would anyone hear her?

The faint sound of music from the tavern drifted toward her. *Nope…probably not.*

She also kind of felt like she was being watched. *Paranoia? Maybe.* The tickling at the back of her neck had her scrunching her shoulders, and she picked up her pace all the same.

"Where's this Reuben guy everyone is talking about?" she whispered to Mr. Whiskers, but he didn't say anything back. He just purred in his contented kitty way. No fucks given.

The cat house was only about thirty feet ahead, if that. The urge to bolt the rest of the way poked her from all sides, but she was scared that if she did that, she'd drop the cat or freak him out enough to make him claw his way over her face.

Just one more alley to cross. She moved a little to the center of the street, putting some distance between her and the black maw of nothing on her left.

As she crossed the alley, she heard a noise. Low and quiet at first, it was a rumble of sound that she didn't know quite how to place. It froze her in her tracks, though. There was definitely a menacing tone to it, like a warning. A growl.

"Do you hear that, Mr. Whiskers?" She couldn't keep the quiver out of her voice. *Keep walking.*

Mr. Whiskers stopped purring. In fact, he stopped moving and was frozen in her arms, his body rigid as he stared down the alley, a murmur of a hiss growing in his belly.

The growling from the alley came again. It was definitely not friendly. *Oooooh nooooo…*

Something dazzled, a blink of light, then twin orbs of blue appeared to be floating in the darkness. *So pretty.* The slow grind of gravel under foot, deliberate careful movements, didn't bring Lucki any comfort. "What is that?"

She unlocked her knees then took a step back. Then another. The sound got louder. The growl grew in strength with each step toward her until it was a warning she couldn't ignore. She moved back quickly, almost stumbling on her own feet. Out of the shadows came a giant dog, its teeth bared, eyes menacing.

No, not a dog.

A wolf!

"H-h-holy shit," Lucki stammered.

The wolf crouched, ready to pounce.

I'm going to die.

Mr. Whiskers hissed a growl of his own then leaped from her arms and she, the stupid fool, chased after him — right up to the wolf, within feet of the menacing beast. Mr. Whiskers stood between them, his fur fluffed out and back arched. He gave a hiss of warning with a paw raised, ready to strike.

"Mr. Whiskers, are you nuts?" Her voice was barely loud enough for anyone to hear. It was a croak instead of a scream. No one would come to her rescue. "Help!" Her voice failed her once again, coming out as a half whisper, strangled by her fear. The wolf watched her, its eyes searing deep inside. It ignored the cat completely.

What is the right move? Why didn't I research this?

What to do if a wolf stalks you…yeah…that.

The wolf took a menacing step in her direction, its predator glare never wavering. Lucki's legs shook with an alarming sway. Her knees were literally knocking together. If she tried to run, she'd fall flat on her face for sure.

Running with a predator giving chase was probably not a great idea anyway.

The cat launched itself, jumping toward the wolf.

Her voice unlocked. "Mr. Whiskers, *no!*"

But it was too late. The cat struck a clawed paw against the wolf's muzzle, causing it to growl and lower its head. Lucki thought for sure Mr. Whiskers was gonna lose all nine lives in one go, but Mr. Whiskers didn't get the memo on that. He struck again, quick and determined, a claw swipe against the wolf's nose.

Lucki quickly calculated the odds of snatching the cat up as she ran. It didn't look good. She was not that coordinated.

She sucked in a deep breath, then opened her mouth to scream.

The wolf took a step back, its head bowed…in…submission?

What the…? Her scream died on her tongue.

Mr. Whiskers, still all puffed out, still defending his human, was no longer on the attack. He even seemed to have a smug grin as he tossed a glance in Lucki's direction. The wolf stayed down, muzzle lowered to the ground, its eyes blinking rapidly.

"Get outta here if you aren't going to be civilized," a booming voice said from behind.

The wolf flicked its eyes up, looked behind Lucki for a moment, then it bolted away into the darkness of the alley.

"Sorry, hon. Got caught up in a conversation and didn't realize you were leaving so soon."

Lucki glanced behind her, then did a double take. A huge, burly man stomped toward her. He had to be at least six-five, six-six. He wasn't wearing a coat, just a blue lumberjack shirt, rolled up at the sleeves, that showed some impressively muscled forearms. His brown hair was parted to the side and his soft eyes crinkled with what kind of looked like amusement. The lower half of his face was covered with a beard, close cropped and well kept. This guy was a bear—a huge, lumberjack bear. He had an easy smile and a dimple, and he was so disarming that Lucki smiled back, that and her panties melted right then and there.

"I'm Reuben." His voice had the kind of husky depth that stroked her soul.

Her legs quivered.

She cleared her throat to get the lusty lump of drool out of the way. "There's a wolf…" She turned her head to the alley, but the wolf was definitely gone. Mr. Whiskers nudged her to be picked up.

"Yeah, I saw." Reuben radiated heat. It literally steamed off him. He came up next to her then placed a firm hand on her back, which instantly steadied her legs. "Let's get you to the house before you freeze to death."

"A wolf, though…" She turned her head from side to side, scanning the area as she bent down to pick up the cat.

"He's gone now. Don't worry about him." Reuben's voice was so sure, so confident, so soothing. "Happy to finally meet you," he added.

"Was that real?" The adrenaline that had coursed through her body crashed out of her in a whoosh. She took a step but her legs crumbled out from under her.

"Whoa there!" Reuben swooped in and held her upright. "They been pouring drinks into you? Those beasts don't ever learn."

Her head was clear. Any buzz she'd had from the booze had burned through her. It had to be shock that was making her dizzy and disoriented now. She could have died. Mr. Whiskers had done his best, but really, that wolf could have eaten her in a few bites.

"I got ya." Reuben picked her up then cradled her and the cat in his arms.

She gasped, more to herself, as she looked up at him. "You're a big guy." She was in the arms of a mountain.

He chuckled. "I am." He hitched her up higher. "Let's get you home, shall we? Then we can properly introduce ourselves. It's Beltane, you know, a good night for introductions." He smiled, his dimple popping and his eyes glistening.

His wink to follow undid her completely.

About the Author

Angela Addams is an author of many naughty things. She believes that the written word is an amazing tool for crafting the most erotic of scenarios and likes telling stories about normal people getting down and dirty and falling in love. Enthralled by the paranormal at an early age, Angela also spends a lot of her time thinking up new story ideas that involve supernatural creatures in everyday situations.

She is an avid tattoo collector, a total book hoarder, and loves anything covered in chocolate...except for bugs. She lives in Ontario, Canada in an old, creaky house, with her husband, children and four moody cats.

Angela loves to hear from readers. You can find her contact information, website details and author profile page at https://www.totallybound.com

Home of Erotic Romance

Sign up for our newsletter and find out about all our
romance book releases, eBook sales and promotions,
sneak peeks and FREE romance books!